4 1/2 Friends

and the

Secret Cave

Joachim Friedrich

Translated from the German
by Elizabeth D. Crawford

First American Edition
1 3 5 7 9 10 8 6 4 2

Printed in the United States of America

Library of Congress Cataloging-in-Publication Data
Friedrich, Joachim, 1953–
[4 1/2 Freunde. English]
4 1/2 friends and the secret cave / Joachim Friedrich; Translated from the German by
Elizabeth D. Crawford.
p.   cm.
Summary: A lonely boy named Radish Rademacher hopes to become a member of his twin sis-
ter's detective agency after showing the members an old treasure map he found in a cave.
ISBN 0-7868-0648-6 (trade)
[1. Friendship—Fiction. 2. Brothers and sisters—Fiction. 3. Twins—Fiction. 4. Buried treasure—
Fiction. 5. Mystery and detective stories.] I. Title: Four and one-half friends. II. Crawford,
Elizabeth D. III. Title.
PZ7.F91515   Aae 2001
[Fic]-dc21   00-46173

Visit www.hyperionchildrensbooks.com

For Susanne

Contents

A Strange Discovery

CHANCE IS A FUNNY THING. If I hadn't been so afraid of Collin seeing me with a baby stroller, I might never have made my secret discovery. But maybe it would be better if I started at the beginning.

It was at lunchtime, right after school. Dad had just made himself his first open-faced tomato sandwich. He did it to avoid Mom's famous hot-dog-and-lentil soup, and tomatoes were all he could find in the fridge. He was holding the sandwich in front of his face, with spread fingers, like a waiter with his tray, studying it warily. I could see his face through the heaps of onion on the slices of tomato. He didn't look very happy. That's because he was going on again about his favorite subject—Dad's a teacher, a math teacher, but not at our school, luckily. All the same, he's always bugging me to study more.

"Can't you at least put down the comic book at meals, Austin? If you must read while you eat, you should be doing something for school instead—like your sister."

I was going to tell him that I'd finished my homework ages ago because I did it in school and that Steffi read comic books, too, but he never gave me a chance.

"In fact, where is Stefanie?"

"Where else would she be? She's sitting in front of her computer—as usual. Steffi!" I bellowed as loud as I could. Miss Grimm, who lives next door, would probably complain about me again. But that would be nothing new, either. If she hears even the tiniest little sound from us, she's standing there at our door, complaining. But it's my parents' fault. Not only did they move us out to the suburbs, but they *had* to pick out the house right next door to Miss Grimm's.

"Austin! Please, not so loud. You know. . . ." Mom rolled her eyes in Miss Grimm's direction. Then, as she filled our bowls, she added, "If Steffi can't be punctual at meals, she'll just have to eat her soup cold." She sat down with us and stared for a few moments at her bowl. "Why is it that I always go to so much trouble to fix meals?"

2

"That's another thing," Dad went on. "Stefanie spends much too much time at the computer."

I was glad my parents had found another subject to discuss, even if it still had to do with the differences between Stefanie and me. At least they were leaving me alone. The thing is, Steffi is really okay. We almost always get along with each other. Only, our parents don't get that.

"It is inconceivable to me how twins can be so different," Dad said, as he cut an onion into many little cubes, all the same size.

"They're fraternal twins."

"I'm not talking about their looks. Although I'm always amazed that Stefanie is almost a head taller and so much stronger than Austin. But you only have to watch them eating to understand why— Austin, please don't nibble your hot dog all over like a rabbit—but what's even more upsetting . . ."

But, lucky for me, Dad didn't get a chance to finish his tirade, because just then Steffi came into the room. She threw her favorite jacket (the one with the Microsoft logo) over the back of the chair, sat down, and reached for her spoon and the bread basket at the same time. If there's anything that can lure Steffi away from her beloved computer, it's food.

"Hi, I'm here! Why didn't someone say lunch was ready? Mmm, lentil soup."

She polished off her first helping faster than a seal with a herring. Only then did she honor us with a glance. "Is something wrong? You all have such weird faces." Mom and Dad said nothing. I just kept nibbling.

Dad seemed to be in a bad mood. Maybe his students had annoyed him. Anyhow, he kept going. "If you aren't going to do any homework, you can at least help in the yard."

I stared at him. That's all I needed! Yard work! Besides, it's the exaggeration of the century to call our doormat-size patch of grass a yard.

Luckily I had a good excuse. "I have to baby-sit Bobby!"

"The Hansen kid?" Steffi sniffed. "Don't you have anything better to do?"

I didn't. Furthermore, it was none of Steffi's business.

"This has nothing to do with you!" I yelled at her, louder than I really meant to. I guess I *am* a tad sensitive about being the only guy I know who baby-sits.

"Don't you yell at me like that!" she yelled back.

"Now, stop fighting, you two," Mom cut in. "And please leave your brother alone, Stefanie."

"Why just me? After all, Radish started it!"

"Please, Stefanie!" Dad huffed. "Don't call Austin 'Radish'!"

Okay, now I have to explain two things: In the first place, everyone calls me Radish, except for grown-ups, of course. How I got that name is very simple. Our last name is Rademacher. And because I'm not exactly a giant, some wiseguy in my class started calling me Radish.

I didn't think it was particularly funny at the time, but everyone else must have, because the name stuck. Steffi even calls me that. I've given up trying to get her to stop.

In the second place, I sometimes baby-sit Bobby. He's the Hansens' kid. They live in the house next to us on the other side from Miss Grimm. Bobby is little—still in diapers—and I don't mind watching him, as long as nobody in my class sees me doing it. Mrs. Hansen pays pretty well, and comic books are expensive. Besides, it breaks the monotony when Steffi's sitting at her computer and I don't know what to do with myself.

When we moved out here to the suburbs three months ago, at first I thought it was great. There were fields, meadows, and the forest right close by. "Many people would envy us," Dad said. But after about four weeks, I knew it was absolutely no good. At least Steffi and I didn't have to change schools. That was a small consolation.

Dad was all excited from the beginning. He'd

always wanted to have "a place of his own," as he said, and he'd grown up right in the neighborhood. However, he didn't like it at all that I was baby-sitting so much. "Can't you find anything else to do with your time, Austin?" He was always nagging me about it. I was getting so I didn't even really notice it anymore. But this time he must have hit a raw nerve in Mom. She let a hot dog fall onto Stefanie's plate with a loud plop.

"Now that's enough! Will you stop nagging the children!"

Dad looked up from his onion pieces in aston-ishment. When Mom used that tone, even Steffi stopped eating. "What do you mean?" Dad asked innocently.

"I mean that you should have some faith in your children. They know what they're doing. If Stefanie is interested in the computer, we shouldn't stop her. She'll certainly be able to use it later. And I think it's very good, as well, for Austin to mind the baby. That can only help you men. . . . Besides, you probably had your own kinks as a child too."

"What's that supposed to mean?"

"Sometimes one has discussions with one's mother-in-law about her husband's childhood," said Mom with a grin.

Dad flushed. "That has nothing to do with this!"

Steffi was about to say something, but she didn't get to it because our doorbell rang. It seemed to go on forever. Dad had insisted that we get a doorbell that could be programmed with more than twenty different melodies. This month it was "Original Big Ben."

Mom waited until the doorbell stopped ringing. "Now who could that be?"

"Probably Miss Grimm complaining again," said Dad. "Austin, please see who it is."

Of course me, I thought, as I went to door.

But it wasn't Miss Grimm. When I opened the door, however, I knew the day was ruined for me. Standing there before me was Collin. He's at least a head taller than Steffi—what that means in relation to me I would rather not go into—plus, he's the best in our class in sports.

"Hi, Radish!" he greeted me, grinning. He thumped me on the shoulder and pushed me aside. "Is Steffi here?"

He didn't wait for an answer but marched straight into our kitchen. He knows his way around at our house. He's here often enough, unfortunately. He turns up at least twice a week, hangs around Steffi, sponges food off us, and gets on my nerves.

Steffi looked up from her lentil soup. "Hi, Collin! So, how many crooks have you caught today?" she said with a grin. My parents nodded pleasantly to him. Otherwise they scarcely took any notice of him. For them he almost belonged to the family, he was here so often.

"Would you like to eat with us?" Mom asked him. At the same time she opened the kitchen cupboard to get out another bowl. Collin had never said no to this question. "Sure! Love to!"

Mom put a bowl in front of him and stirred the ladle around in the soup pot. "Strange. I could have sworn there was still a hot dog in here."

Steffi's grin broadened. "Maybe someone stole it. A new case for Collin and Co.: the disappearing hot dog."

"I don't know what your problem is," growled Collin, looking longingly at the soup pot. "After all, you belong to it too."

That got Dad's attention. "What do you belong to, Stefanie?"

"To Collin's detective gang," I answered for my sister.

Collin raised his index finger. "Detective agency, Radish. Collin and Co. Detective Agency."

"Detective agency. My, my."

Mom and Dad looked at each other. Their expressions didn't change, but I thought Mom winked at Dad.

"Do you belong to it too?" Dad asked me.

Collin didn't give me a chance to answer. "Radish? Nah. More likely he's a Dinosaur."

Dad choked. "Dinosaur? Excuse me?"

Collin made a face. "There are a few guys in our class. Total crackpots. They call themselves the Dinosaur-Man Gang."

"And do you hang around with them?" Dad asked.

Now it was Collin's turn to choke. "Are you kidding? With them? Do you know what they do? They bring their plastic dinosaur dolls to school and play with them during recess. Basically, they shove them back and forth in front of them and yell 'Zap!' and 'Bang!' and 'Owww! Got me!' Is that stupid, or what?"

Dad sat there, his partly eaten tomato sandwich in his hand, listening to Collin with his brow knitted. "Uh—oh—yes," he said finally. "And what do *you* do in your spare time?"

"We solve criminal cases."

"Really?"

"Oh, well, we're still practicing. Nothing ever happens here. Now, if we were in New York—"

"By the way, I have a new computer game," said Steffi, interrupting Collin. "It's called Treasure Hunt. We can try it out if you want."

Collin scraped up the last of the lentil soup in his bowl. "Treasure Hunt? Is it like a training program for detectives?"

"Sort of."

"Then what are we waiting for? Let's try it!"

I knew which game Steffi meant. Only two could play that one. And it wasn't hard to figure out who would get to be the onlooker. I was already considering what I could do alone when Big Ben thundered through the front hall again. Dad looked up.

I didn't let him get a word out. "I'll get it," I said and went to the door. It was Mrs. Hansen. She smiled pleasantly at me. She always did that when she wanted something from me. "Hello, Austin," she said, after she had briefly looked over my shoulder into the house. "I'm glad you answered the door. I wanted to ask you something."

"Do you want me to watch Bobby now?" I said.

She nodded and smiled even more pleasantly. "Exactly. My husband and I want—"

I didn't let her finish. I turned around, fished my jacket out of the closet, and pulled the front door closed behind me. I didn't want Collin finding out about my baby-sitting Bobby. Steffi had sworn to me that she wouldn't tell him anything about it. Luckily, I can rely on my twin sister.

"This is really nice of you, Austin," said Bobby's mother, beaming. "You're really helping us out."

"It's okay," I replied magnanimously. After all, I couldn't say to her that I was broke and just needed the extra money. Besides, I'd rather play with a toddler than sit around letting Collin get on my nerves.

When Bobby saw me, he squealed with pleasure. Whenever Bobby realizes I'm going to take him for a walk, no one can restrain him. He waddles between the front door and the kitchen, back and forth without stopping. And because he can't really walk right yet, he stumbles every ten steps at the most, sits down on his padded bottom, then stands right up again. The scream that he lets out each time is almost unbearable.

Mrs. Hansen hurried to get his things together. She stuffed it all into the net on the back of his stroller as quickly as she could, with the commotion Bobby was making. She had to put Bobby in first to do it because all the stuff that we had to take was so heavy that without him in it, the stroller would tip over backward.

I was nervous, so Bobby's screaming really got to me. I didn't under any circumstances want Collin to see me with the stroller. He'd be sure to tell everybody in the class about it tomorrow, and I didn't even want to imagine how much I'd be teased then. I always went out the Hansens' back door when Collin was at our house. I have a regular route when I go out with Bobby: down our street, then right along the field path through the meadow, past Farmer Beckman's farm, across the little brook, around through the forest, past the pond and the big clearing, until we come out on the other side of our street again. All in all, it takes about an hour. After that we go back to the Hansens' and I play with him. Translation: I chase him around, making sure he doesn't break anything.

I walked very slowly. After all, I had lots of time. The forest is, as I said, very close by and pretty big. Because it's so close to the city, on the weekends it's full of hikers. But you hardly meet anyone on ordinary weekdays.

"Can you imagine that my dad played here when he was a little boy?" I asked Bobby. He looked up at me and beamed. I like to talk to Bobby—at least he doesn't interrupt. Besides, he likes it when you talk to him. I went along the forest path and imagined Dad and his friends jumping out from behind the trees. I would have liked to do that too. Only I would have needed a couple of friends to do that, and I didn't have any here. Only Bobby.

The forest was thicker than it looked from a distance, almost creepy. It was very still. Even Bobby was sitting quietly in his stroller. Maybe he found it creepy here, too. "What's the matter, little guy?" I asked him. "Are you scared?" This time he didn't look up at me. He sat there motionless in his stroller and sort of stiff.

"Hey, what're you doing?" The question was unnecessary. Suddenly, I knew what was happening. Bobby's ears got red and he let out an unmistakable sound. I smelled the result of his efforts immediately. He was facing into the wind. At first I tried not to pay any attention. That didn't work for very long.

"Gross, Bobby! You stink!"

"Da! Da!" he replied, and beamed again as if he had broken a new world record.

What should I do? On the one hand, the stench was almost unbearable, on the other hand there was no decent place nearby to change a diaper. I decided to pick Bobby up and walk a little deeper into the forest with him. I parked the stroller against a tree. When I picked Bobby up and grabbed the bag with the diapers, he began to cry. He hates to be changed. And I hate to change him. I considered whether I ought to charge Mrs. Hansen more.

I'd headed pretty far into the forest, when I saw a mossy clearing in front of a rock wall. That was a good place. On that day, with only Bobby as my

13

witness, I think I broke the speed record for changing a baby. After I finished, I looked around wondering what to do with the dirty diaper. Obviously, I couldn't take it with me. On the other hand, I couldn't just throw it away. I'd heard something about environmental protection, after all. So I had at least to get rid of the contents. They were fully biodegradable, so to speak.

Holding my breath, I spread the bushes apart. It was then that I saw a hole in the rock wall. It was big enough for my head to fit through it. It was a tiny cave! I looked around. At first I couldn't see much. There was just a little light coming through a crack in the wall. It was really creepy. A small shaft of sun was shining on an outcropping of rock.

I was looking directly into two pairs of glittering eyes.

A Real Case

I CROUCHED IN FRONT OF THE CAVE, rooted to the spot, staring at a doll and a teddy bear. What were a doll and a teddy bear doing in a hidden cave? There was definitely a story behind this—there *had* to be.

I grabbed Bobby, turned, and dashed away. I had to tell this to the two superdetectives. After all, this was something different from a computer game—something real. There were a couple of stones lying right beside the mossy area, and of course, clumsy as I am, I stumbled over them. I performed an almost circus-perfect acrobatic maneuver as I fell. If I hadn't rolled so skillfully, Bobby would have been squashed under me. When I'd managed to get to my feet again I checked to make sure none of my bones were dislocated. And then, as I bent once more to pick up the diaper, I had an idea.

Steffi and Collin were sitting at the computer when I got to her room. Before my discovery I'd been wishing Collin would disappear as quickly as possible. Now I was glad he hadn't left yet.

"What's the matter, Radish, back already?" Steffi greeted me as I stood in the door with Bobby in my arms. "Hey, what's the matter with you? Why are you just standing there? Do you want to play?"

On the way back I'd figured out what I was going to say to Steffi and Collin about my discovery. And now I was standing there in front of them and didn't know how to begin.

Collin didn't make it any easier for me. "What's the matter? Why are you looking so weird? And what's that kid doing here?"

"That's our neighbor's boy," Steffi answered for me. "Austin baby-sits him sometimes."

Now he'd found out after all. I'd completely forgotten about that. His comments came fast and furious. "Baby-sitter? Really? How sweet! Mom Radish!" he roared, hammering his fists on Steffi's computer table with delight.

I didn't have to defend myself. Steffi took over the job. "Idiot," she hissed as she examined her table. "If you've broken my table, you're a dead man."

16

Collin grinned in embarrassment. I think he even blushed. "Don't worry. Come on, let's keep playing!"

The time for my big news had finally arrived. "I don't think you should play anymore."

Steffi turned back to me. "Why not?"

I waited a moment before I answered. That increased the tension. "I discovered a cave."

"Uh-huh," said Collin without taking his eyes off the screen. "So?"

"There was something hidden in it. And I found it." That did it. Both were looking at me wide-eyed. It was so cool!

"Well, don't keep us hanging!" cried Steffi. "Say what you found, for goodness sake."

I held it under her nose. "This."

Steffi raised her eyebrows. "A dirty old piece of paper? Is that what you're making such a big deal about? I think you've flipped."

"Dirty old piece of paper my foot!" I yelled at her, so that Bobby jumped and began to howl. I had to quiet him down again before I could go on. Steffi and Collin watched me the whole time without saying a word. They seemed to be very curious. That was good.

"So, now, what's with the piece of paper?" Steffi asked when Bobby was again quietly playing with his squeaky duck.

"It's a treasure map." I said it very casually. I

didn't look at either one of them. They could come to me if they wanted it. And they came. With one leap they were beside me, peering over each of my shoulders.

"Treasure map?" asked Collin. "Really? Let's see it!"

"As I just said. It was stuck in a cardboard box. Looked very inconspicuous. But when I unfolded the paper, I saw what it was." I held the map under Collin's nose. It was really cool. His eyes widened.

"Oh, crazy!" cried Steffi. "Is it real?"

I shrugged my shoulders. "Don't know."

Collin put on his expert's expression. "Of course it's real. Anyone can see that. Here, hand it over."

He grabbed for my hand. But I was faster and pulled it back. "No way! Look yes, touch no!"

Steffi gave me a sisterly clap on the back that took my breath away. "Oh, Radish! Don't be that way. At least give it to me. Or don't you trust me?"

I trusted that Steffi would give it back. Nevertheless, I hesitated a moment. But finally I gave it to her. After all, she is my twin sister. Collin was beside her the moment I handed it over. He bent down closer to the map. She could have pinched him in the nose. Unfortunately, she didn't.

Collin was turning his head like Miss Grimm's dog when somebody holds a piece of sausage out to him. "It says something. What does it say?"

Somehow he reminded me of those guys in the

Westerns. They always gasp for breath like that when they're dividing up their loot.

Steffi read it out loud: "It says January fifteenth, nineteen fifty. Man! Then it's already—wait a minute." She counted back on her fingers. "It's more than fifty years old by now!"

"Exactly!" I cried. "There was a really old, genuine treasure map in the cave! The first time I didn't see it at all. But then I went back again."

Collin and Steffi went totally out of their minds. I had to tell them every detail about how I'd discovered it. It wasn't so easy, though, because I had to fib a little bit.

"Bobby got away from me," I lied. "He ran into the woods and crawled in behind some bushes. I ran after him and then I discovered an overgrown cave entrance." I thought Collin already knew enough about Bobby and me, so I didn't say a word about the full diaper. I glanced over at Bobby. At that moment he was busy pulling apart one of Steffi's comic books. Luckily, she didn't see it.

But Steffi and Collin weren't even interested in how I had discovered the cave. Their minds were fixed on the map.

"And what about the map? Was it just lying there, or what?"

"I just told you. It was in a cardboard box. That's

probably why it lasted so long. But there was something else, too."

"Something else?" Steffi interrupted. "What?"

"A doll and a teddy bear."

Steffi and Collin were looking at me as if I weren't quite right in the head.

"A doll and a teddy bear?" Collin repeated like a parrot. "Like a baby doll for playing and a stuffed bear?"

"Yes, that's what I just said."

Steffi shook her head. "Are you trying to put one over on us, little brother?"

"Baloney! Why should I lie to you? After all, the map seems to be real, doesn't it? There was a doll and a teddy bear! They were sitting on a little outcropping, staring at me. It was totally creepy!"

"So why didn't you bring them with you?"

"Because they were completely cruddy. They smelled really moldy, just like the cardboard box. It almost fell apart. Only the map was okay."

"Man, Steffi!" cried Collin. "We were just playing treasure hunt on our computer. And now we have a real treasure map. Cool!"

"How do you intend to find out if it really is a treasure map?" Steffi asked suddenly.

"Of course it's a treasure map! Come on, Steffi, let's see it again!"

She spread the map out on the desk. There was a

double line drawn on it that wandered from the top to the bottom in loops and windings all over the page. At both ends of the line was a fat black cross. There were strange signs and a few numbers beside them.

Steffi and Collin stared for quite a while at the yellowed piece of paper. Steffi scratched her head. "All the same," she mused, "I always imagined a treasure map very differently. I mean, with more clues to the treasure. There are just numbers and signs on this thing. The only thing you can recognize is that this funny worm between the two crosses could be a path."

"But that's a treasure map!" cried Collin. "It's obvious. And there, where the cross is, that's where the treasure is hidden."

Steffi leaned back. "Okay, wiseguy. And which one of the two crosses do you mean? And where are they? There isn't anything about it on the map."

Collin shrugged his shoulders and looked sheepish.

I didn't want to give up before we'd even started. "But this path must exist somewhere!"

"Somewhere! Of course it's somewhere. But where?"

Collin pulled the map over to him. "The most important thing is for us to proceed systematically. After all, it would be ridiculous if we couldn't crack such a stupid code."

Collin was probably one of those children Mom talked about: the ones who are allowed to watch too much television.

"Crack the code?" I asked. "Like how?"

"How should I know? You think of something once in a while. Do I have to do all the work myself?"

"I think I already have an idea," said Steffi, ignoring Collin. "Radish found the map in a cave, right?"

"Yes. So?"

"So perhaps one cross is the cave."

"Then we only have to follow the path that's drawn from the cave right to the—"

"Would we really find a treasure?" whispered Collin, as if he were afraid someone could hear us.

I didn't know why he was so excited. If there actually were a treasure, then it would probably belong to me. After all, I had discovered the cave.

"Of course there's a treasure there," I said lightly. "Why would anyone draw a map like this if there weren't? Only I'd like to know what it has to do with the doll and the teddy bear."

That kept running through my head the whole time. A cold shiver went down my spine when I thought about them sitting there, staring at me. I wasn't exactly comfortable with the thought of going back again, but I didn't say that to the two of them. I could do without more dumb remarks from Collin.

"Do you want to go there again?" I asked as casually as I could.

"Well, sure!" cried Collin. "What do you think? If one of the crosses on the map is actually the cave, then we have to go there. Get it?"

"Of course I get it!" Collin was almost acting as if it were his treasure. "It isn't a crime to ask a question, after all."

"No, it isn't," Collin said magnanimously. "Now, back to the map. Maybe you overlooked something. Maybe we'll find another clue that sheds light on the mystery of the doll and the teddy bear."

Sheds light on the mystery! He'd do better to shed light on his brain once in a while.

"Just look at the date!" he prattled on. "Nineteen fifty—that's really old."

"Sure is," Steffi concurred, as she bent over the map again. "And I'll bet the marks that are drawn on the left and right of the pencil line represent specific clues on the path, number of steps or something like that."

"Number of steps! Exactly!" Collin interjected. "Steffi, you're a genius!"

"And the marks at the other end are certainly distances, probably paces."

"Exactly!" roared Collin again. "Now it's almost straight ahead!"

"Well, children. Are you diligently solving criminal cases again?" Suddenly Dad was standing in the doorway.

It is unbelievable! Grown-ups knock on doors everywhere except their kids' rooms.

"We? Um . . . nothing, I mean . . ." I stammered. I decided to keep my trap shut or he would become even more curious.

It was too late. He craned his neck. Fortunately, I was able to make the map disappear in time.

He came over to the desk. We looked up at him and he looked down at us. He stood there that way for a while, looking.

"You're hiding something from me!"

"Radish, I mean Austin, discovered a cave!" cried Steffi.

I didn't mind that she'd told about that. Dad was curious. That meant that he wouldn't let it go until he'd found out what he wanted to know.

"A cave?"

"Yes! Isn't that cool? And a doll and a teddy bear were in it, too!"

Good one, Steffi! She only told him half of it. He would certainly be satisfied with that.

"What was in it?" he asked once more.

"A doll and a teddy bear!" I cried. "Really, Dad. That's it."

"We were just saying that we want to examine the cave more carefully," Collin explained.

For crying out loud! How could he say that? I knew exactly what was coming next.

"Under no circumstances!" my dad declared.

There, you see? I do know my father.

"But why not?" asked Collin. He didn't know my father as well as I do.

"Because I don't want you running around in the woods alone. It's too dangerous."

"But Dad!" I tried once more. It didn't do any good.

"You're not to go. Is that clear?"

Steffi nodded. "It's clear, Dad. We won't go."

I knew very well what that promise was worth. But Dad believed it.

"Well, then, good."

He was about to turn and go. Then his glance fell on Bobby, who was just beginning to enjoy his second comic book. "That reminds me why I came in the first place, Austin."

"Why?"

"Because you're supposed to take the child home. It's already late. Dinner is ready. Mrs. Hansen has even phoned already."

That was the cue for Steffi. "Can Collin eat with us?"

I was to be spared nothing. Naturally Bobby also screamed as if he'd been stabbed when I separated him from his beloved comic book. And when Steffi saw what he'd done, I got to hear some more from her, too.

I picked up Bobby, along with his diaper bag, and made tracks to the Hansens' as fast as I could.

Mrs. Hansen didn't really look as though she'd been waiting for me. Dad had probably just said that so that I would take Bobby home. I found that Dad had a tendency to exaggerate. I knew, after all, that he had a problem with me baby-sitting. He would have preferred me to be with boys my own age.

Luckily, I had Mom on my side. I'd been going to the refrigerator one night recently, and heard Mom and Dad arguing. Mom shouted angrily. "If Austin wants to baby-sit the boy, then he should do it! I'm not going to get into it. And I'd be grateful if you didn't either."

"All right, all right," I heard Dad murmur apologetically. I'd felt better at the time, but unfortunately it hadn't done much good after all.

Dinner went peacefully, anyway, in spite of Collin. We told Mom about the cave. Dad didn't say anything more. He shoveled his food in without looking up from his plate.

Mom didn't make as big a fuss about it as he had. All she said was, "Oh, really? How nice."

But she would probably also have said that if we'd told her that King Kong was sitting in the living room in front of the TV eating peanuts. She never worried about what Steffi and I did except when the neighbors complained about us.

Collin took off pretty quickly after dinner. But I heard him and Steffi making plans at the front door. "And tomorrow after school we'll go over this cave a little more thoroughly with a magnifying glass," he whispered.

To be honest, I didn't like that at all. That night, as I lay in bed and couldn't get to sleep, I decided to make it clear to Collin who the boss of the treasure hunt would be.

Next morning, when I got to the schoolyard with Steffi just before school, the other partner in Collin's detective agency was standing there with his boss. Norbert. He was listening to Collin attentively. I smelled trouble.

Steffi had similar thoughts. "I'll bet he's talking about the treasure map."

I just nodded because I was busy preparing the

words with which to tell Collin that I wanted to lead the treasure hunt.

"Hi, Steffi —hello, Radish," the master detective greeted us.

"What tales have you been telling already?" Steffi greeted him back.

"I've just explained the situation."

"What did you explain?"

"Oh, well, I just told Norbert that Radish discovered a cave and a . . . "—he craned his neck and peered around as if some kind of secret police might be lurking around the area—". . . and a treasure map," he whispered. "Come on, Radish, give it here."

Norbert gave me a look that I couldn't read, exactly. But still, I thought there was something like admiration in it. It felt very good.

That's probably why I had the courage to actually say to Collin what I'd planned to: "Hey, Collin, I just want to make sure you understand that I want to be the leader of the treasure hunt."

"You want what?"

"To be the leader of the treasure hunt."

"What?"

I cleared my throat. "I mean, I discovered the cave, so I want to decide how the treasure hunt goes. You can advise me, of course, and tell me if you agree with my plans. But until then I'm not showing the map to anybody."

I didn't feel as brave as I sounded. I stood there and stared at Collin. He stared back like someone who has heard something unbelievable.

What Steffi and Norbert were doing, I didn't know. I looked neither to the right nor to the left, only at Collin's face. Although the yelling and screaming in the schoolyard was certainly no softer than on any other normal morning, I felt as though it were dead quiet.

Four and a Half Friends
and No Dog

I DON'T KNOW HOW LONG we stood there just looking at each other like that. For me it was an eternity.

The school bell rang once. That meant we had seven minutes to get to our classrooms. Normally I hated that prison racket, but this time it was a kind of relief. "So, now you know how it is," I said, and I turned around and went up to the door as fast as I could without looking as though I were fleeing the scene. I was glad when I could finally take cover in the pushing, squealing crowd.

When I got to my classroom, I was the first to arrive. I slung my jacket onto one of the hooks by the door and sat down. I rooted around in my book-bag, and after a long time I pulled out my biology book, although I'd found it at the first grab. I started reading it without seeing what I was reading. I wouldn't even have noticed if the book had been upside down. Luckily, Steffi—who sat next to me—didn't come in with Collin and Norbert until right after the second bell. She still hadn't sat down when it became very quiet. Ms. Hober-Stratman, our biology teacher, had arrived. That saved me from having to talk with Steffi.

Ms. Hober-Stratman began telling us something about the inner workings of pigs. On other days, this would have bored me to death, like most of the stuff in bio. I would have shot spitballs or written notes like the others. But I listened, fascinated, to how the digestive system of the pig functions. I even raised my hand. After the third time, Ms. Hober-Stratman raised her eyebrows in astonishment. But I still kept on paying attention.

Between first and second period I wasted time digging around in my book bag again, tidied up my already tidy pencil case, and looked at every schoolbook possible without reading a word. We had geography second period, studying the oil deposits in the North Sea. Again, I was riveted. When the bell rang for morning recess, I could hardly believe it. The first two periods had gone much faster than usual.

The end of school was the opposite of the

beginning. I was the last one out of the classroom. I slunk along as slowly as I could, but it didn't do any good. I reached the main door and looked down into the schoolyard. They were waiting at the foot of the big stairway. Collin and Norbert were standing next to each other and looking up at me. There was no way to get past them. Steffi was leaning against the wall, somewhat off to the side, her arms crossed over her chest. She looked like an observer who was expecting a good show.

I went down the steps slowly. I must confess that my knees were like jelly. When I was still two steps away from them, Collin cleared his throat.

"We have something to discuss with you, Radish."

"Yeah? What is it?" I asked, and I had a lot of trouble making my voice sound moderately normal. Just don't croak, I thought. That's always what happens to me when I'm especially excited or afraid.

Collin gestured over his shoulder with his head. "Not here. Let's go to the bicycle stands. We won't be disturbed there."

He turned around and trotted off. Norbert ran behind him, just like a good partner. Steffi and I brought up the end of the procession. I would have loved to ask her what Collin wanted from me. But she kept looking stolidly straight ahead, so I didn't talk to her. I had my pride too, after all. I did wonder why she was grinning, though.

When we were standing in the farthest corner of the schoolyard, Collin made a proposal that nearly bowled me over. "We were conferring a while ago. And we almost unanimously decided —"

"Almost?"

"Well, so to speak. Anyway, I've decided to take you into our detective agency as a partner."

I looked at Steffi, but that didn't help me at all either. She had again assumed her observer posture and grinned at me.

"Yes, uh," I stammered. "I don't know what to say."

Collin thumped me patronizingly on the shoulder. "Don't say anything, pal."

Norbert gave a grunt.

"However, there's still one little problem," Collin went on with a sidelong glance at him.

"Problem?"

"Yes. The case. Norbert thinks that you should still have to solve one case before you're accepted, just like the rest of us."

Oh, man! Anything but a case like the ones he and Norbert had solved! In fact, I wouldn't even call them real cases. It had all started when Collin happened to see someone stealing a bicycle from the schoolyard. Collin followed the thief without his seeing him and then told the principal where he'd gone. That way the police had been able to catch the thief quickly. That was when Collin decided to open his detective agency.

"So, you want to be accepted, or not?" Steffi asked suddenly.

"Oh, well, I don't know. What do you think about my having to solve a case?"

"You already know what I think about that. Utter baloney! As far as I'm concerned, you don't have to solve a case."

"Well," Collin said. "*I* think Norbert is right. No case, no partner. Anyhow, not for men."

Of course! He'd already made an exception for Steffi. Probably just so he could come and use her computer. Of course, the others in our class thought Steffi was Collin's girlfriend, but I knew there was no possibility of that.

"Then I won't be a partner," I said. Where I got the courage, I have no idea.

"Dude!" cried Norbert. "But what about the treasure map?"

"You can forget it."

"Perhaps there's another way then," said Collin. "How would it be if it were enough to find a treasure map. Make that the case, so to speak. But of course I would remain the boss. That's obvious."

Aha. So that's how it was going to be. I really had no idea what to do. I'd have preferred to forget the whole thing, but then I'd be making a complete fool of myself.

"What's this about a treasure map?"

Startled, we whirled around. It was Nicky, the leader of the Dinosaur-Man Gang. He was standing just two yards away. We hadn't noticed him sneaking up on us.

Collin's ears turned red. "Treasure? What treasure? And what are you looking for here anyhow, you jerk?"

"Hey, who're you calling a jerk, jerk? You think you own the schoolyard? So what's this about a treasure map?"

"What treasure map?"

"Dude!" Norbert interjected. "It's nothing—just a new case."

Nicky grinned at him. "You and your dopey detective game. Kid stuff!" He turned around and went back to his gang members, who were waiting for him at a safe distance.

"And your plastic junk?" Collin yelled after him. "That isn't kid stuff? Zap, zap! Bang, bang!"

"Do you think he believed me?" asked Norbert when Nicky was out of hearing.

Collin shrugged his shoulders. "No idea. In any case, we'll have to be super-careful in the future or they'll snatch the treasure from right under our noses."

"Is Radish a partner now or isn't he?" asked Steffi, who could hardly hold back her laughter.

"Agreed?" Collin asked me. I nodded.

"Dude!" cried Norbert. At that very moment the bell rang. The break was over.

On the way back to our classroom I walked beside Steffi again. "I haven't even had a chance to eat my snack," she complained. "Anyway, I'm proud of you for what you said to Collin."

"Really?"

"Really."

I'll say it again: Steffi is a first-class sister.

"But you're a boy and so you're also crazy."

Oh, well, sometimes she's still a little difficult.

The next two hours of school went just as fast as the first two. Only this time it was for a different reason. Collin had taken me on as his partner! Perhaps we would actually find out what the doll and the teddy bear were all about. In return I'd have to tolerate him as boss. I'd have to think carefully about that. That took the next two hours. This time, though, I hadn't the slightest idea what the teacher talked about. But that probably didn't matter too much because we had history and music. The more I thought about my dealings with Collin the more pleased I was at how everything had turned out.

When the bell rang for the next break, I left with my new detective friends. Collin steered us straight over to the bike racks again.

"We have to watch darned carefully," he said after the usual inspecting look. "Nicky's certainly already told his men that we've got something big in the works. I don't know how much he could have heard when he was snooping around here before. Maybe they even know about the cave already."

I felt as if I were in a film. "And what are we supposed to do?" I asked him.

"Be careful, very careful, Radish."

"Dude!" cried Norbert. "Let's make some plans finally!"

"Plans? What plans?"

"When we're going, what equipment we need, what clues we're following . . . the whole thing."

Norbert never calls anyone by his name. To him everybody is "Dude!" And it's all the same to him whether he means his friends or his parents, pupils or teachers, grandma or grandpa, uncle or aunt, children or grown-ups. Norbert is about as tall as I am but he makes up for it by being twice as wide.

And he's always up for anything. So, of course, he was into solving a case for the detective agency. For example, he got into Collin and Co. by spying on our bio teacher because she went into the map room so often. "That's very suspicious," he said. One day she opened the door suddenly while he was hanging around in front of the map room waiting for her. Man, can she glare, that Ms. Hober-Stratman. She singed Norbert into a little pile of ashes with one look, and with that the Hober-Stratman case was closed. "Actually that's not a real case," Collin had told Norbert. "But I'll accept you anyway."

He was probably glad that someone had at least tried to solve a case.

Norbert would have preferred to cut the last periods and get started immediately.

"All right, then," said Collin, "we'll make some plans. Do you have the treasure map with you, Radish?"

I pulled it out. That took some time, though, because I had stuck it in the wallet I wear around my neck. Norbert jumped impatiently from one foot to the other, as if he had to go to the bathroom. When I'd finally fished the wallet out from under my sweater, shirt, and undershirt, I took out the map and gave it to Collin.

Norbert immediately grabbed it. "Dude! Cool! What's all that supposed to mean?"

We briefly explained to him what we'd figured out the day before.

"So then we'll go to this cave right after school, right?" he asked when we were done.

Collin shook his head. "Not right away. We'll all go home first, just the way we always do. Our parents mustn't get suspicious. Besides, then we'll confuse our enemies, in case they're following us." He looked at each of us, one after the other. "Anyone have any objections?"

We had none. It sounded quite logical, although I was beginning to believe that Collin was suffering from a persecution complex.

"When do we meet, then?" Norbert wanted to know. Collin scratched his head. "Let me think for a moment. School is out at one. We need half an hour to get home. Luckily we don't live too far away from each other."

That was true. Collin's parents had also bought a house in our development and Norbert lived only a few streets farther on.

"Okay," Collin kept on figuring. "We don't need longer than half an hour to eat. And if we tell our parents that we don't have any homework to do, we can meet at two-thirty at Steffi's——I mean at Radish and Steffi's. Then we still have half an hour to spare in case something goes wrong. All clear?"

Again we nodded. It did sound smart. I began to think that Collin really was a good detective boss.

Norbert asked, "And what about equipment?"

"Where do you think we're going, anyhow, Antarctica?" Collin said, rolling his eyes.

"A shovel wouldn't be bad," Steffi observed. "After all, you said the treasure is buried somewhere. Or do you want to dig with your hands?

"No, of course not. All right, good, we can take a shovel. Who's going to bring it?"

"Always the one who asked," said Steffi with a grin.

Collin sighed. "All right, then, I'll provide that, too. I think there must be one lying around in the garage. Is everyone okay with that?"

We were. Nevertheless we kept on talking about a few details. For example, we considered where we'd hide the treasure, what our parents would say, and how we'd divide the money, once we had dug up the treasure. We agreed that we'd each receive the same share. "Fifty-fifty for everyone," as Norbert put it.

The last two hours passed without any particular incident. We had English, which is an easy subject for me.

I was in a good mood on the way home. Steffi and I talked without stopping about the cave and about Collin and Co. Normally we walk along next to each other pretty quietly. What is there to talk about when you see each other every day? But this was no normal day. There are some days that begin rotten and then turn out to be really fantastic, I was thinking. But what I didn't think about was the fact that it can be the other way around sometimes, too.

When we got home, Mom was there alone. Normally Dad would have gotten home before us. He'd called Mom and told her he'd be coming later because he had to go to a teachers' meeting that he hadn't known about ahead of time. So we could talk with Mom while we were eating without Dad's getting all excited again.

"Mom?" Steffi asked when she'd hardly swallowed her first bite. "What was it like around here around fifty years ago?"

My sister rarely minces words. I almost choked.

"My goodness, Stefanie! What questions you always come up with! Why do you want to know that?"

"Oh, Mom, please just tell. It's for school."

She can lie, that Stefanie. Man!

"What do you mean, exactly?"

"Well, what was it like here in our

41

neighborhood? We're particularly interested in whether there were maybe some very rich people living here."

Mom looked at us skeptically. "Do you have to know that for school too?"

Steffi and I nodded. Two of us lying works much better than one.

"Well, I can't really say that exactly. I wasn't born until later. But this much I do know, it was mostly farms, so there were only a few people living here. And they were not rich. As you know, Dad lived close by as a child. If you want, I can ask him about it when he comes home."

"Better not, Mom," I said quickly. "That's not necessary."

I preferred not to get Dad involved in this. Certainly he'd immediately think of the cave.

"Who else could tell us more about it?" Steffi asked.

"Grandma and Grandpa, of course—and the other people who lived here at the time. Only I don't know what their names were or where they're living now."

We couldn't talk about it anymore. Big Ben had sounded.

It was Norbert, ten minutes ahead of time, naturally.

"I couldn't wait anymore," he said. "So I came a little early."

We'd hardly pulled the door closed behind us when Collin showed up too. As promised, he had a shovel with him. It was gigantic and totally rusted.

"What's that monstrosity you're dragging with you?" Steffi greeted him.

"You certainly can ask dumb questions! I was supposed to bring a shovel. My grandfather used to use this to put coal in the coal bin."

That's what the thing looked like, too.

"Dude! I think it's great! You can dig really big holes with that. After all, we don't know how big the treasure is."

"You can carry it, then," said Collin and he pressed the shovel into Norbert's hand. "Now, can we get going?"

I'd been putting it off until the last moment, but now I had no other choice. "Can you wait a moment?"

"What now?"

"We have to take Bobby with us."

Steffi let herself drop onto to the little antique telephone bench that stood in our hallway. "No way!"

"Who's Bobby?" asked Norbert with his usual intelligent look. "Another new partner?"

43

"It's a little boy I sometimes baby-sit. But he can be very useful. In fact, he was there yesterday when I discovered the cave."

Steffi was still sitting on the little bench. "Is it really necessary?"

"Yes. I promised Mrs. Hansen a week ago. Besides, I'm broke."

"But—"

"Oh, let it go," Collin interrupted my sister. "As long as we don't have to change him, he won't bother us."

I didn't wait to hear Steffi's answer but ran off to get Bobby. While Mrs. Hansen was putting his junk together, I saw through the window that Steffi, Collin, and Norbert, with the rusty shovel over his shoulder, were waiting in front of the house. So Steffi couldn't be that mad about it. And I could only marvel at Collin's behavior.

"Da, da!" Bobby greeted Collin and Co., when we came out of the house. Steffi looked at him warily but at least she didn't complain about it.

We took the same path Bobby and I had taken when we discovered the cave. On the little bridge, right behind Beckman's farm, Norbert stopped, raised the shovel from his shoulder, looked over the bridge railing into the water, and sighed.

Steffi stopped and looked back at him. "Is the

shovel too heavy for you, Norbert?"

"No, no, I just thought of something."

"Yes? What?"

Meanwhile we had all gone back to Norbert and were standing around him.

"Now we're almost just like the five friends."

"Like the five what?"

"Dude! Don't you know them? That's the famous detective gang. There are tons of books about them."

"What are you babbling about?" cried Collin. "Say, are you having a romantic attack or something? We're real detectives, man. Five friends! That's just kid stuff!"

"That's not true at all. No, honestly, they really are almost just like us."

"How would four and a half friends be?" Steffi cracked, with a glance at Bobby.

"You are totally idiotic, you know?" Norbert snapped. "Besides, we don't have a dog!"

"What's that got to do with it?" Collin wanted to know.

"Because detective gangs like that always have a dog! Don't you know anything at all?"

"We could take Miss Grimm's dog," Steffi suggested. "But then you'd have to carry him as well as the shovel."

Norbert didn't think that was very funny. He put Collin's family heirloom back on his shoulder. "You'll see that we'll solve just as many cases as the five friends. Then you'll come and beg me on your knees to tell you about them."

He turned around and marched on ahead without favoring us with another glance.

He would probably have gone on like that for hours if I hadn't called him back. "Hey, Norbert, we're there!"

In an instant he forgot that he was offended. "Dude! Really? Where's the cave?"

"We have to go into the woods a little ways."

"So let's go," said Collin. "You go first, Radish."

I did. I must admit that I loved having the three of them following me for once. Now I was the boss, in a way. If I hadn't had to carry Bobby, I would probably have gone a longer way around. I enjoyed it that much.

"It's there, behind the bushes," I said when we were standing almost in front of it.

Norbert reacted the fastest. The shovel flew between the trees in a high arc and at the same time he flung himself on the bushes. He bent them apart and stuck his head inside the crack in the rock.

"You can't see anything in here," he groused.

Steffi shoved him aside. "Let's see."

Norbert obediently stood up. Steffi knelt in front of the hole and looked at it from all sides. After quite a while she stood up and turned to us.

"No wonder you didn't see anything, Norbert. There isn't anything to see. The cave is empty, except maybe for a few spiderwebs."

Treasure Hunt with Stumbling Blocks

COLLIN WAS AT THE CAVE in one leap. He stuck his head so far in that I thought he'd disappear inside. When his face reappeared, it was flushed. Without a word he stomped past me onto the path. I'd rather not describe the look he gave me as he went by.

But that wasn't possible! I put Bobby down on the moss and looked myself. They were right! The crack in the rocks was empty. I could not believe it. I had definitely seen the doll and the teddy bear!

When my eyes got a little more used to the dark, I saw an old scrap of material lying on the floor. The doll and the bear had probably been sitting on it. I picked it up to show it to Collin and Norbert and Steffi. But they'd already vanished between the trees. I wanted to catch up to them, so

I hurried out of the bushes and tripped over that darned stone again. I almost landed right on it, nose first. I raised my eyes and thought I must be dreaming. First the doll and the teddy bear had disappeared and now this. Could Collin have been right? Was there really a treasure? When I reached over to pick it up, my hands were trembling worse than during the last math test.

I grabbed Bobby and ran. It was a miracle I managed to get back to the path without taking another bellyflop.

Collin, Steffi, and Norbert were waiting for me.

Norbert even had the shovel on his shoulder again. Their faces were not very friendly.

Silently, I stowed Bobby in his stroller. I couldn't have said anything anyway. I was panting like a marathon runner.

"There wasn't anything there at all!" Collin snapped at me. "Were you kidding us or what?"

"I wasn't," I panted. "The doll and the teddy bear were there when I discovered the cave. Honest! Here, I found this scrap of material. But—"

"Oh, yeah? Give it here!" Collin took the scrap, looked briefly at it, and immediately stuck it in his pocket. "Who knows where you picked up this old rag? All right, tell me where the doll and the teddy bear are *now*."

"I don't know. But——"

"Did they just vanish into thin air? Or did they maybe come to life and run away?"

"Now just let him finish what he's trying to say," my sister defended me.

"Well, all right," said Collin, drawing a deep breath, "Then talk!"

I was still completely out of breath. Besides, I couldn't explain what had happened. So I held under Collin's nose the thing I'd been clutching firmly the entire time.

"Man! What's that sup——" The word literally stuck in his throat. He only stared at my hand.

"Man, Radish! Is it real?"

Instantly, Norbert and Steffi were beside us.

"Crazy!" cried Steffi. "A coin! Where'd you get it, Radish? Was it in the cave?"

"In front of it. Only a few yards away from the entrance."

"It's got to belong to the treasure!" Norbert whooped. "C'mon, let's go back again. Maybe we'll find some more of it!"

He would definitely have thrown his shovel away again, but Collin held him back.

"Take it easy, Norbert. First we have to examine the coin very carefully."

Before I could stop him, he'd grabbed it. Steffi

immediately took it away from him again. She examined the coin on both sides. She turned it back and forth, held it up to the sun, and hefted it in her hand. I wouldn't have been surprised if she'd bitten it.

"It's heavy! Much heavier than an ordinary coin. And look how it shines! It's gold. It's simply got to be gold!"

Collin was less excited. "Does it say anything on it?" he asked, sounding slightly offended. It probably wounded his detective honor to have Steffi just take the coin away from him that way.

Steffi looked at the coin again. "Yes, it has something on it. Wait a minute. Ten German *marks,* nineteen-twelve, and an engraved letter—an E or an F, I think."

"Nineteen-twelve?" cried Norbert. "Dude, that's much older than the treasure map."

"So what?" Collin said. "Someone could still have buried it later."

Steffi shook her head. "If one cross on the map is supposed to mean the cave and the other means that the treasure is buried there, why would the coin have been lying in front of cave? It would have to've been lying at the place marked with the other cross, wouldn't it?"

Collin dismissed that with a wave of his hand. "How do I know! Radish found the coin in front of the cave. So first we should check there to see if we find anything else. We can always worry about the other cross later."

"So what should we look for?" I asked.

"For instance, for a hole that was just recently dug out, for some fresh soil, et cetera, et cetera. What you could find anyplace a treasure has been dug up. But somehow I hope we don't find anything like that."

"Why not?"

"Man, because then the treasure is gone! You still have a lot to learn, Radish."

"I still say that we should look for the treasure here!" cried Norbert, and he went rushing off. Collin and Steffi were right behind him.

"And what about the doll and the teddy bear?" I cried. They didn't hear. They probably weren't interested. Their heads were full of the coin. I picked Bobby up and went back along the path to the cave. I wracked my brains to think what it could have to do with the coin. Where were the doll and the teddy bear? It was inexplicable! If we found a treasure now, too, I would crack up!

We didn't find any treasure. We looked under every bush, turned over every stone. Norbert even crawled around the forest floor on all fours. Nothing.

"There's no point in looking anymore," Collin said finally. "There's no treasure here. Let's go back to the path."

"What'll we do now?" I asked our boss when we again stood around Bobby's stroller.

"We have to look in the place where the other cross is drawn on the map," Steffi answered for him.

"All right, then," growled Collin. "Hand over the map, Radish."

For the third time that day I rooted around in my wallet. Once more he carefully examined the pathway marked out on it. "It's very simple, see. If this cross here is the cave and the other cross the treasure, then we only have to go on along the path we came on. Get it?"

Steffi, Norbert, and I looked at the map and nodded. "The first sign after the cross looks like a tree," Steffi said. "So we have to look out for a special tree."

The tree wasn't hard to find. It was gigantic and must have been ancient. There wasn't a single leaf left on it. The other signs on the map were also easy to decipher when you saw them in reality for the first time: a large clearing, a pond, and a place where several paths crossed one another. With each sign we discovered, we exulted as if we'd already found the treasure.

I knew the path we were walking on. It was exactly the same route through the forest that I always took with Bobby. Finally, we came to the edge of the forest and were standing at the end of our street.

"Now only the numbers are left: ninety steps straight and twenty steps to the right!" Steffi cried, and she was off and running.

Suddenly she was back again. She came over to me and plucked my sleeve. "Do you know where our treasure is?"

"No, how should I? Where?"

"Dude! What's wrong? Let's go!" cried Norbert. He'd already begun running, still carrying the shovel.

"C'mere!" Collin called him back. "Something's wrong here." Norbert came bounding back.

"What's the matter?" he gasped as he came up to us. "You looking at that house there?"

"Miss Grimm's house," I answered for Collin. "There are five steps more, at most, up to the house."

"So?" asked Collin.

"But according to the map there are still fifteen steps left to the cross."

"Then the treasure is in your neighbor's yard?"

"Absolutely right."

"Isn't that the old witch who's always complaining about every little thing?"

"Of course," said Steffi, sighing.

"So?"

"I'm not going in that yard!" I cried. "After all, I'm too young to die!"

"Dude! It probably won't be so bad. After all, she isn't a real witch."

"You can't be so sure of that," said Steffi. I could only agree with her.

"You didn't miscount, did you?" Collin asked carefully.

"You can check me if you don't believe me!"

We checked it, "Just in case," as Collin said. Of course he didn't look at Steffi as he said it. My sister had not miscounted. The cross on the map indicated the left rear corner of Miss Grimm's yard.

"Dude! What are we going to do now?"

"Simple. We'll call a conference to discuss the situation," our boss informed us. "At Steffi and Radish's." He looked around at Steffi. "Is that okay?" he asked just in time.

Steffi exhaled noisily. "All right, I don't care. But the shovel stays outside!"

Norbert dropped it on the sidewalk with a clatter. "Nothing would please me more. Where shall I put it?"

"You can put it in our front yard. It won't bother anyone there."

Mom stuck her head out of the kitchen as we came in. "Hello, children. Did you find lots of beautiful treasures?"

"Why didn't you put an ad in the newspaper?" Collin hissed at me as we went up the stairs.

Steffi suggested holding the discussion of the situation, as Collin called it, in her room. "Perhaps we can use my computer," she said.

We sat on Steffi's bed and the two little armchairs.

"Don't you have anything to drink? My throat feels like the Sahara after all that schlepping around," Norbert groaned.

We got soda and glasses from the kitchen, gave Bobby his juice bottle and a comic book, and made ourselves comfortable. I thought it was really cool being a detective.

Collin cleared his throat importantly. "Okay, let's get started with our discussion of the situation."

"Discussion of the situation! What idiocy!" cried Norbert, interrupting him. "We'll go down to her yard, dig up the treasure, and be done with it."

Collin clapped his palm to his forehead so hard that it smacked. "Man, Norbert, if stupidity squeaked, you'd have to run around all day with an oil can! If we just go into her yard and Grimm surprises us, she will certainly scream to the whole neighborhood. Then they'll all come running and ask us what we were digging there for. And what do you say then? Well, what do you say then?"

"Okay," said Norbert sulkily, "but you shouldn't have said that about the oil can."

"All right, then. I'm sorry. So now can we make a plan for how we can get at the treasure?"

Nobody objected.

"Good. Then I'll take suggestions."

He didn't hear any suggestions because none of us could think of anything clever.

Norbert's idea of abducting Miss Grimm's dog so as to lure her out of the house was rejected. She took care of Waldo better than I took care of the gold coin.

"How would it be if we simply asked her?" our boss suggested.

"Do you have a bulletproof vest?" replied Steffi, nixing that idea.

"I think I just got an idea of what we should do," said Collin. "Your suggestion wasn't so bad after all, Norbert."

"You see? Oil can? I don't think so!"

"We can't abduct the dog," Collin mused, without paying any attention to Norbert's remark. "But we could distract her somehow anyway."

"Somehow?" asked Steffi. "What does that mean?"

"I don't know exactly yet. Don't you have any idea about what's guaranteed to make her react?"

"Noise!" Steffi and I cried at the same time.

"Dude! I know. One of us makes so much noise in front of the house that she comes out and chases him. And in the meantime the others can dig up the treasure in her backyard in peace."

Collin looked at Norbert. "I take that back about the oil can, Norbert."

"That's what I said."

"And who's going to play decoy?" I wanted to know.

"It would be better if it were one of you two. She knows you."

"And which one of us?"

"You—that's probably obvious."

Of course! I ought to have seen that coming. "But Steffi can run much faster than I can," I pointed out.

"How about if we both did it," Steffi suggested. "We make noise together. She knows that."

"Does anyone have any objections?" Collin asked.

I certainly had some when I thought of Miss Grimm, but I kept still. After all, nothing better had occurred to me, either.

From the hallway we called in the direction of where we thought Mom was that we were going outside to play. It's always good to say that. Then the parents don't get suspicious.

Before we went out, Collin softly repeated the plan of attack of "Operation Witchhunt," as he named our diversion maneuver. "So, Norbert and I slip around your house and penetrate the yard from behind. Steffi and Radish go out in the street in front of the house and make noise. What are you going to do?"

"She hates soccer playing and yelling the most," I answered.

"I'll get the ball," Steffi cried.

While she whisked down to the basement, I put Bobby in his stroller. He could watch us playing soccer. I hoped he wouldn't get scared when he saw us yelling at each other. I pressed a cookie into his hand for security.

The shovel was still lying in our front yard. Norbert grabbed it and he and Collin slipped along the little pathway that led between the houses to the yards behind. Steffi and I went out front, to the street, as if we actually intended to play soccer. I pushed Bobby's stroller close to the hedge so he wouldn't be in the way. We kept kicking the ball back and forth and almost screaming our throats out. "Can't you look out, you dope?" and "Where do you think you're kicking, you jerk!" and "Goal! Goal!" and "Are you blind? That was no goal, no way!" Bobby looked from one to the other and screamed excitedly in between.

With all the noise, we didn't have to wait long before we saw a shadow at the window. The flowered curtains were pushed aside and Miss Grimm's sharp nose came into view. "She could break a balloon with that nose," Steffi had said once.

I was standing at an angle with my back to the window, so I could only observe Miss Grimm out of the corner of my eye. But I felt her gaze on my back. It bored through my jacket and my T-shirt right down to my skin. That must have been the way Hansel and Gretel felt when they were trapped while they were eating the witch's gingerbread house. I wouldn't be surprised, I thought, if Collin and Norbert were to find a fattening shed and an oven in the backyard. Anyway, I was looking forward to what the two would have to tell. I didn't know what Miss Grimm's yard looked like. Shortly after she moved in, she had the entire thing enclosed with a wooden privacy fence. The walls were at least six feet high. We couldn't even see anything from our upstairs windows. There a tall, dense evergreen tree obscured the view.

I slowly grew hot. In the first place, playing soccer and screaming at the same time is very strenuous, and in the second place that stare was still burning into my back.

Finally she opened the window and let off her usual volley of scolding: "This is just outrageous! There are other people living here who have a right to peace and quiet! Is that the way your parents bring you up? It's like a kindergarten out there!" She says that to us quite often. I guess to Miss Grimm kindergarten is the most horrible place in the world because there are a lot of children there who make a lot of noise. She should come visit us at school sometime.

Steffi and I were just about to let go with a few fresh remarks when we saw a shovel coming around the corner. Steffi threw the ball into our front yard, I took the stroller and Bobby, and we ran behind Collin and Norbert. They ran as if Miss Grimm was after them. We didn't stop until we got to the end of our street.

We had to catch our breath for a minute before we could say anything.

"What's up? Did you find the treasure?" Steffi gasped.

"Not quite," Norbert gasped back. "Man, is this stupid shovel heavy! And all for nothing."

"Not quite? For nothing? What's that supposed to mean?"

"It means we don't have the treasure," Collin answered for Norbert. "But that's probably obvious."

"What's in the yard?" I finally asked.

"A shed."

I thought I'd misheard. "A shed?"

"Shed is an exaggeration," Collin said. "It's more a kind of a rabbit lean-to. There were two bunny rabbits sitting in there and they were goggling at us as if we were the wonders of the world."

"Exactly. And beside this shed there's a huge mountain of firewood piled up."

I remembered that Miss Grimm had told people that she'd had an open fireplace built.

"So?"

"Very simple. According to our reckoning, the treasure must lie right smack under this pile of firewood. We can't get to it!"

Secret Investigations at City Hall

"SHOULD WE JUST GIVE UP?" I asked.

"Give up? Are you crazy? No way. We just have to have another discussion of the situation."

We checked to make sure we could sneak back to our house without Miss Grimm seeing us. Luckily the coast was clear. The window was closed and the flowered curtains were hanging in their usual perfect folds.

Norbert threw the shovel into the front yard and we went into the house. We sat down in Steffi's room again, just as we had for the first discussion of the situation. Bobby even got the same comic book again. Only it wasn't quite so much fun this time around. In fact we sat there feeling pretty depressed.

"Don't you have anything to eat?" Norbert asked. "A person works up an appetite with all that running around. And I'm thirsty, too."

I got another bottle of soda and two bars of chocolate out of the kitchen. The mood rose again as soon as we'd fortified ourselves.

"So," said our leader, "let's go over the problems we have once more."

"You do it," Steffi said with a grin. "You can do it best."

"Uh, yes, all right," Collin stammered. It's really cool how Steffi only has to make one remark and the great Collin is completely flabbergasted.

"It would be best if you start with 'all right, then,'" said Steffi, adding to his misery.

"What? Aw, c'mon, quit it, Steffi. All right, then—I mean, we found the cave, but the teddy bear and doll were gone. Then we discovered where the treasure is hidden, but we can't get at it. Furthermore, we don't know what this treasure is at all. Of course we have the gold coin, but that was lying in front of the cave. I'm wondering whether your neighbor hid the treasure under her woodpile herself."

Steffi shook her head. "I don't think so. She moved here the same time we did. Certainly she had no idea what was lying there under her yard."

"You're right," said Collin, "we can't get any further this way. We have to ask somebody who used to live here before."

"My grandparents," Steffi suggested. "They used to live in this area."

"Why did they move away?" Norbert wanted to know.

"Haven't a clue. We could ask them though."

"We should leave your grandparents out of it," Collin interrupted Steffi.

"How come?"

"Too dangerous. I don't even think it's good that you got your parents involved. If we turn up at Grandpa and Grandma's now, too, some sort of suspicion's going to arise, for sure. And you know how it is when grown-ups start asking curious questions."

"Well then, what do you suggest, O Great Master?"

"First we should interrogate the people who won't immediately ask the whys and wherefores. If that doesn't get us anywhere, we can still always consider visiting your grandparents."

"And just what people do you have in mind?" I demanded.

"Officials, so to speak."

"Dude! You mean police or something like that?"

"Nah, we don't have to go running to the police

right away. I was thinking of City Hall. They're always collecting files about everything possible."

"But where do we start? City Hall is enormous."

"How do I know? We'll ask around until we find the right department."

"And if they won't tell us?"

But we couldn't worry about Norbert's questions any longer because suddenly we heard a terrible racket downstairs. It was Dad.

"Who left this monstrosity in the front yard?" he bellowed. He was talking to us. That was obvious.

"Let's go down fast and get rid of the thing before he totally flips out," said Steffi.

Dad was standing in the hallway. He had Collin's family heirloom in his hand and he was snorting with rage.

"Does this thing belong to you?"

"Yes, Dad," I said. "We were treasure hunting with it in the yard."

"In the yard? You weren't digging holes in my yard?"

"No, certainly not, Mr. Rademacher!" cried Collin. "We were just about to go. And we'll take the shovel with us!"

Norbert ran down the steps behind Collin. "I have to go home too. So long! See you in school tomorrow!"

The two of them had never disappeared so fast as they did that day.

Dad had calmed down somewhat by dinnertime. He didn't even complain when he saw that I was watching Bobby again. The baby, meanwhile, had fallen peacefully asleep over his comic book.

At breakfast the next morning Dad went on the rampage again and insisted that I was bolting down my cereal, so Steffi and I were late leaving. Collin and Norbert were waiting for us at the school gate, their faces reproachful. "You're just showing up now? You know we have a lot of work ahead of us today."

"Calm down," Steffi replied. "Radish needed time to finish his breakfast."

I was going to protest, but Collin wouldn't let me. "Let's talk about important things now," he said pompously. "We have to discuss when we're going to meet today to go to City Hall."

"Is it open this afternoon?" Norbert asked.

"All checked out, partner. It's open."

If Collin inflated any more, he'd explode. I was just about to say that to him, when someone smacked me so hard on the back it took my breath away.

"Well, master detectives. You solving the perfect crime again?"

It was Nicky again, the Dinosaur leader, who had sneaked up behind us without our noticing.

"You're playing with fire, you know that?" Collin snarled at him.

"Don't act so big," Nicky sneered back. "Are you still searching for treasure? You'll never find it, you know that, don't you?"

We were so stunned that none of us could say anything, not even Collin.

"Dude! How did he know that?" cried Norbert when Nicky was back among his gang of friends again.

Collin shook his head. "Haven't a clue. But I don't like it. I don't like it at all."

Unfortunately the bell had already rung for the second time and we had to go in to class. I couldn't get Nicky's remark out of my head. Could the Dinosaurs have taken the doll and the teddy bear from the cave? Did they have anything to do with the coin? I couldn't imagine that any one of them owned something so valuable. The whole story was getting more and more mysterious.

The others weren't any wiser than I was. As much as we talked during the break, we couldn't figure out what Nicky had meant by his remark. Finally Collin said, "Let's just go to City Hall. Perhaps we'll still find out something that will help us."

Luckily, the teachers had mercy on us that day as far as homework was concerned. So Steffi and I got out of the house and had no problem getting to City Hall at the appointed time. We were even there early. But Collin and Norbert didn't keep us waiting long.

Our boss immediately took command with "Let's go in and get to work."

In the reception room, he confidently walked right over to the information window. I was curious to know what he would say.

We stood for a while in front of the glass window until the guy at the desk noticed us. He opened a little round speaking hole. "Yes?"

"Good afternoon," our boss began.

"Afternoon. What d'you want?"

"Well, it's rather complicated."

Mr. Information raised his eyebrows. "Just try me, kid. Maybe I'll understand it anyhow."

Some grown-ups can be really encouraging. Steffi shoved Collin aside.

"We have to write a composition for school," she lied.

"You don't say! And?"

She went on. "It's got to be about how things used to be in our city."

"Used to be? What does 'used to be' mean?"

"Fifty years ago."

"Aha. And what do you want to know about that? How it looked here? Even I could tell you that, you know. It was all farmland. In those days I was—"

"No, no!" Collin interrupted. "It's more about who lived in our section of the city."

Mr. Information scratched his chin. "Oh, well, the residents' registration office is really responsible for that. But I don't think they'll tell you anything. It's forbidden to reveal information about other people, y'see—here in City Hall, anyway."

"We'll try it anyway!" said Steffi, beaming at him. "Where is this office?"

"Room one-oh-one."

We left it to Collin to find out where Room 101 was. "This could be fun if it goes on like this," Norbert whispered to me as we made our way down a long corridor behind Collin. I hoped he was right.

The entrance to Room 101 was a gigantic set of double doors. Behind them we could hear voices murmuring and phones ringing. It wasn't very inviting. My heart was bumping in time as we went in. Inside we stood before a counter that was so high that even Collin had difficulty seeing over it.

An old woman with gray hair pulled into a knot on top bent down over us. "What can I do for you,

70

children?" she asked, friendlier than she had appeared at first look.

Steffi told her the composition story. At the end she added another "Oh, please, help us" to it.

"I'm really sorry, children," said the woman with the knot. "I'm not allowed to give you such information."

"If you don't help us, we're certain to get a zero!" cried Norbert.

I was afraid that was overdoing it a little. But it worked!

The friendly woman looked at us sympathetically and sighed. "Where do you live, then?"

We gave her our address. She looked around once to see if anyone was watching and then began tapping on her computer.

"Let's see," she said to the monitor screen. "I'll just look. I can't promise you anything, because really, what I'm doing isn't allowed. But I already told you that."

Steffi stretched her neck so as not to miss anything.

"What period did you say you have to write your essay about?" the knot-lady asked suddenly.

"Nineteen-fifty," Steffi replied.

"Tsch, then I can't help you even if I wanted to."

"Why not?"

"Because the street you just named for me has only been there a few years."

Collin clapped his hand to his forehead. "Man! Are we stupid! Of course our streets weren't there then! Before our houses were built there were only fields. At least that's what my parents said."

We looked at each other. "So what should we do now?" I asked her.

"Try to find out which are the oldest streets in your neighborhood. Then come back and I'll see what I can do for you."

She felt sorry for us, that was obvious, so at least there was a good chance of finding out more.

So I asked, "Where can we find that out?"

"You could try in the land registry office. It would be best for you to ask for Mr. Lautenbach. He's nice. Give him my best regards. Room two-sixteen."

We thanked her politely and made our way to Room 216. Collin took over the leadership again.

The door of Room 216 had a notice that said PLEASE KNOCK BEFORE ENTERING!

That was not a good sign.

We knocked. Three times. When we still didn't hear any "Come in," Steffi opened the door and went in first. At the window stood a man with his back to us, busy with a watering can among the potted plants on the windowsill.

"Can't you knock?" he fumed at us.

"But we did!" cried Norbert.

"Okay. And? What do you want?"

"Are you Mr. Lautenbach?" asked Collin.

"No, Mr. Lautenbach is not here. Are you relatives of his?"

"No, we're not, but we have to write a composition about what our neighborhood was like fifty years ago," Steffi recited for the third time. "And so we want to know what streets were there then."

"Do you want to inspect the files of the office?" Norbert tried. "No, no. We merely want to peek."

"Peek!" cried the man armed with the watering can. "Well, now I've heard everything! The records are off limits to 'peekers.'"

I would have liked to run away, but at that moment the door opened and an older, fatter man pushed his stomach in. "Ah, you're here already," he said with a pleasant smile.

The man with the watering can looked at the fat man in horror. "Do you know these children, Mr. Lautenbach?"

"No. At least, not yet. But I met our nice colleague Ms. Stubbs from the residents' registry office in the hall. You know, she always has that strange hairdo that looks like a bird's nest. She told me that

73

a few children were coming who wanted needed some information."

"They want to inspect our files!" Watering Can was getting excited again.

"Keep cool, Mr. Smyth," said Mr. Lautenbach drily. "How about taking a little break? Go have a cup of coffee or something. I can manage things here."

"But Mr. Lautenbach! You wouldn't let anyone . . . ?"

"Just let me worry about that."

"I trust you know what you're doing, Mr. Lautenbach!" He set his watering can down on the desk with a loud smack and stalked out of the room.

"Is he always like that?" asked Norbert.

"Yes. It takes a while to get used to him. Luckily he isn't in a bad mood today. Then he's *really* unbearable."

"Will you help us then?" Collin asked.

"Well, we'll see. If I understood my colleague correctly, you want to know something about the area around Farmer Beckman's farm."

"You know him?" I cried.

"Certainly. I lived there once myself. I came here as a very young man when I was not much older than you. Old Farmer Beckman took me in at the time."

"Then you must also know who else lived in the

area back then!" Collin was fidgeting with excitement.

"Sure, sure. There weren't many, though. The houses were quite old and then were torn down when the new development was going to be built there."

"Did any family move away before that?" Steffi asked. "Maybe because they got rich very suddenly?"

"Rich?" said Mr. Lautenbach with a laugh. "No, none of those people were rich. I know that for sure because a good friend of mine lived there. They all lived there because the rents were very low. They only moved away when the houses were going to be torn down. Some went into old-age homes or they found cheap apartments in another part of the city."

"Didn't anything unusual ever happen?" Collin kept trying. "Some kind of mysterious occurrence?"

"Occurrence? Mysterious? Hmm. That I might have known. . . . That is, wait a moment. Now that you mention it, there was something. I was still living with Farmer Beckman at the time."

"Really?" cried Collin. He almost leapt at the man.

"Then again, it wasn't really so mysterious," said Mr. Lautenbach. "I can remember that one family did move away quite suddenly. No one knew exactly why, or where they went, either. When anyone asked them, they never wanted to say specifically. They would only say there were personal reasons."

Collin dug in his pocket and pulled out a little notebook and a ballpoint pen.

"Would you also tell us what those people's name was?"

"Wait a moment—it's on the tip of my tongue. They had a little boy, that I still remember. . . . Now I have it! Rademacher. Their name was Rademacher!"

Lunch with Surprises

WHEN WE GOT OUTSIDE, we sat right down on one of the benches that were placed all around the City Hall Square. "Is it possible that your grandparents buried a treasure?" Norbert asked me. "Are they that rich?"

I shook my head. "No way. They're just regular retired people."

Collin looked at me. "Nevertheless they're the only ones who can be considered to be possible perpetrators up till now."

Perpetrators! What baloney. Grandpa and Grandma were certainly not criminals. I'd have liked to give Collin a piece of my mind. But I couldn't do it. Everything was jumbled in my head. First the cave, the doll, the teddy bear, then the coin, and now this, too! I didn't understand anything at all anymore. Where was all this going to end? Collin and Norbert were looking at me as if they could read in my face what Grandma and Grandpa might've had to do with the cave. Why were they looking at me and not Steffi? And then to top it off, she left. She simply got up and walked away.

"Hey, where are you going?" I called after her. But she just kept on going, without turning around.

"Dude! What's the matter with her?"

"Hearing all that was probably too much for her."

"Oh, come off it, Collin!" I yelled. "You're acting as though my grandparents were major criminals!"

"Aw, come on! Why are you so touchy all of a sudden? After all, you have to admit that the circumstantial evidence—"

"Oh, you're crazy," I interrupted, crossed my arms over my chest, and said nothing more. It didn't last long, because Steffi reappeared. She was grinning broadly.

"What are you so happy about?" Norbert asked her. "Do you know what your grandparents might have had to do with the treasure?"

Steffi's grin widened. "Not yet."

"What's that supposed to mean?"

"That means that we're going to ask them. I just

phoned them. We're supposed to go there tomorrow, for lunch."

I couldn't believe my ears. Not that too! "Why
for lunch, of all times?"

Collin and Norbert looked at me uncompre-
hendingly.

"Dude! What's up? Is your grandma that bad a
cook?"

"Oh, don't pay any attention to him," Steffi said
for me. "He'll calm down. Well then, shall we go to
my grandparents' tomorrow?"

"Sure we'll go!" Collin was in top form again.
"We finally have a hot clue, so we have to follow it.
Agreed, Radish?"

"Fine. It doesn't make any difference now anyway."

"Good. Then we're in agreement again."

"We have go to my grandparents' right after
school tomorrow or we won't make it to lunch,"
Steffi said. "Is that a problem?"

Collin and Norbert looked at one another and
shook their heads. Collin rubbed his hands together
in anticipation. "Good. Then everything is settled.
Are there any more questions?"

I stood up "I've had enough for today."

Collin looked at his watch. "Radish is right. It's
already pretty late. Let's go home."

In contrast to the day before, Steffi and I walked

home without saying much to each other. But at one point I asked her, "Did you really have to call Grandpa and Grandma?"

"Don't you even want to know what they have to do with the whole story?"

I wasn't sure what I wanted anymore. "Sure," I said, nevertheless. "But did it have to be lunch?"

"That wasn't my idea. You know Grandma."

"Yeah."

After supper, when Dad stood up to go see what was on television, Steffi seized her opportunity.

"Oh, Mom, we're going to Grandma and Grandpa's for lunch tomorrow. So you don't have to cook for us."

Mom looked at me. "To Grandma and Grandpa's? Just like that? Or is it still something about your composition?"

"Uh, yes."

It's no fun to lie to your parents. But what were we going to do? We'd started doing it that first time and now we had to keep on with it. Did Mom still believe us? She didn't say anything, of course, but something about the way she looked at us was different from usual.

The next morning in school we talked at each break about what we wanted to ask my grandparents. Collin was in high gear. He kept musing about how we could question Grandma and Grandpa as "discreetly" as possible and nevertheless "extract" as much as possible from them.

Finally we agreed that we would simply ask why they moved when they did.

"But we won't show them the coin under any circumstances!" Collin ruled. "On that point we won't budge at all."

My grandparents lived not very far from school, so we could easily walk there. Of course Norbert complained, but we just ignored him.

Grandpa met us at the apartment door, in a good mood, as always. "Well, there you are, children. Grandma was afraid you'd get here too late to eat."

I looked at the clock. "But we're early."

"Yes, yes, I know," said Grandpa, laughing. "But you know your grandmother. When it's a matter of eating, she has no sense of humor."

Grandma was in the kitchen, as usual. She had on a flowered coverall apron and was stirring something in a pot.

"Oh, there you are, children. Sit right down at the table. The food is just about ready."

Although I can't list them, it seemed to me that Grandma's repertoire of dishes had increased.

"Are we supposed to eat all that?" Collin whispered to me.

"All of it," said Steffi, grinning. "Grandma doesn't like it when anything is left over. So, make an effort. After all, we want to get some information from her."

"The first course is a hearty chicken soup," said Grandma, beaming. She placed a gigantic soup tureen on the table and immediately began ladling the deep soup plates full to the brim.

After saying grace, into which I privately inserted some special requests, Grandpa fired off his usual starting signal: "Enjoy your meal, everyone!"

I knew that you have to attack Grandma's "hearty" chicken soup with extreme caution. The little blobs of fat are so close together that they don't let out steam. Mom always complains that the soup is "deceptive."

Norbert had never encountered deceptive soup before. He immediately started spooning up the soup like crazy. But at the first swallow he dropped the spoon onto the plate with a loud cry, scattering Grandma's chicken soup and fat blobs onto the tablecloth.

Grandpa, who was sitting near Norbert, patted his hand good-naturedly. "Be careful, my boy, the soup is hot."

Norbert was holding his hand over his mouth. "Dude—uh—so I noticed," he muttered.

We got through the rest of the soup without any problems. But the biggest job still lay ahead us: the main course.

We stuffed in as much as we could. Norbert reminded me of a steam shovel. Grandma looked over at him a few times and smiled with satisfaction. I unbuttoned my trousers. I can get more in that way.

Grandma was content. "All eaten up! Lovely that you liked it so much. And now, because you've been so good, you've earned a reward."

She stood up and disappeared into the kitchen. Soon afterward she appeared with a glass bowl big enough to give Bobby a bath in.

"Dessert! Vanilla pudding on fresh strawberries with chocolate sauce!"

I looked at the others. Steffi and Collin looked sort of exhausted. Only Norbert was still in just as good shape as before the chicken soup. One strawberry after another vanished into his mouth.

I began to eat. Little pink spots danced before my eyes. Somehow I managed to get down the last strawberry. It was lying right under my larynx.

Just when I was thinking we'd finally finished, Norbert did something that almost stopped my heart.

He held his dessert dish up to Grandma. "Do

you have any more of that delicious pudding, Mrs. Rademacher?"

Grandma looked at the bowl. It was empty! Grandma had never had that experience with us before. She looked appropriately dismayed.

"Unfortunately, there is no more. But I still have a few bars of chocolate, if you want. Milk chocolate, semisweet, marzipan, almond, or mocha cream—you can choose."

"Mocha cream!" Norbert was beaming. "That's my favorite!"

We sat in the living room. There was cocoa for us and coffee for Grandma and Grandpa. It's always especially comfy with them after a meal. You can stretch out in an armchair and recover. It was just the right mood. I sat with my back to Norbert, though. He was munching away happily on his mocha-cream chocolate. I just couldn't look.

"By the way, there's a reason we came to visit you today." Our interrogation, as Collin called it, began.

Grandpa raised his eyebrows. "Is that so, my boy? What's going on? Are you having problems in school?"

"No, no!" cried Steffi. "It's about something entirely different. We want to know from you what your life was like fifty years ago."

"But, Steffi," Grandma said, "we've told you about that so often already."

"Sure. Only that was always about how little there was to eat and how you went to the farmers to exchange your things for food."

"True. It is important you know about that so you value how good things are for you today."

"We do, Grandma," I said, backing up my sister. "Only, this time we want to know something about your move."

"What move?"

"You used to live in the neighborhood where our development is. And then you moved."

"That's true," said Grandpa. "So you want to know why we moved away from there?"

"Yes, exactly," Collin butted in. "The thing is, we have to write a composition for school."

"About our move?"

"No, not specifically, only sort of in general . . . uh."

Grandma gave him a friendly smile. "Of course, we can tell you. After all, it isn't a secret."

Collin looked relieved.

"Right," said Grandpa. "The reason was your father."

My heart almost stopped again. What did Dad have to do with it?

"Really less your father and more the circumstances under which we lived there. The house was very cheap, to be sure, and really not bad at all—anyhow, for the conditions in those days. But it was quite isolated. Therefore there were no playmates for our son, that is to say, your father. He was alone all day long. And over the long term that wasn't good for him. So we moved to an area where there were children in the neighborhood."

"Not good for him?" Steffi asked. "How do you mean that?"

"We were afraid he'd turn into a loner. We'd already noticed the first signs of it."

"What signs?" I wanted to know.

"As Grandma has already said, there were no children in the area. And it was probably too far for school friends to visit him. However, he often spent hours running around in the forest alone. That gave us a lot to think about in those days."

"In the forest, huh?" said Collin significantly. "That's interesting. What did he do there, anyway?"

Grandma shrugged her shoulders. "He played there. Probably he built tree houses, explored . . . whatever children his age do in a forest."

"Did he also discover caves, perhaps?" Norbert interrupted loudly. "Or did he ever bury something?"

"Oh, are there caves in the forest?" Grandma answered with another question. "And as to whether he ever buried anything, of course I don't know."

Collin poked me in the ribs with his elbow. "Go on, Radish. Show them the coin."

I couldn't believe my ears. I looked at Steffi and Norbert, but they didn't say anything. They were probably just as surprised as I was.

"But you said that we weren't under any circumstances—"

"What coin should you show me, my boy?" Grandpa asked. I could tell by looking at him that he'd gotten curious. What else could I do? I dug out the gold coin and handed it to Grandpa.

"Did you ever see it before?"

He took it out of my hand, looked only once, briefly, at it and gave it to Grandma, who was craning her neck in curiosity.

"Where did you get it?"

"Why? Do you recognize it?"

"Oh well, I don't know if I recognize this particular coin. But when my parents were young, back in Germany, you could spend them in any store—if you had any.

"But that's a very long time ago," Grandma added.

"Can you show me the coin again?" Grandpa asked suddenly.

Grandma gave it to him. He looked at it for a while from all angles.

"I'm not certain," he said finally, "but I think I have seen a similar coin—in your father's hands."

"Dad?" Steffi and I cried at the same time.

"Yes. He once showed it to me and said that it was his good luck piece."

"When?" asked Collin. "How long ago?"

"Oh, it's a few years now. But now tell us where you got this coin. It does appear to be real, in fact."

"I found it," I admitted.

"Where?"

"In the forest, in front of a cave."

It didn't matter now anyway.

Grandpa and Grandma looked at one another. "Aha," said Grandpa with a grin. "So that's what this is about. That business about the composition probably wasn't quite true, eh?"

"White lie," said Steffi.

"You see, we think there's more of it. A treasure!" Norbert babbled.

"It must be buried in the forest somewhere," Steffi added hastily. That was good. That way she kept Miss Grimm from being dragged into it.

"And so you thought . . . "

"And so we thought that you might be able to help us along."

"Children, children," said Grandma with a sigh. "Why didn't you tell us the truth? Were you afraid we'd take the coin away from you?"

"Oh well, probably not that you'd take it away from us but that you'd want to know exactly where we got it and stuff."

"And that we would spoil your detective game. Is that right?"

Collin winced at the word *game*, but he said nothing.

"Well, now we know where you got the coin," Grandpa said. "But what's going to happen to it is much more important. If it actually is real, you must give it back to its rightful owner."

"Before we've found the treasure?" cried Norbert. "But we would so love to get the finder's reward!"

Again Norbert's yammering worked.

Grandma and Grandpa exchanged looks. "What do you think?" Grandpa asked.

Grandma gave us a look I knew. Only grandmas can look like that.

"Very well," Grandpa said, sighing. "I'll make you a proposition. I'll give you two days. If you haven't found any treasure by that time, then ask your father if the coin belongs to him. If it doesn't, take it to the lost-and-found office at the police station. What do you think of that?"

"Three days," said Collin.

"We're not bargaining. Either two days or nothing at all."

"It's a deal," Collin muttered after a brief glance at us.

"And you won't say anything to Dad?" Steffi asked again to be on the safe side. "Not before the two days are up?"

"Promise." Grandpa looked at the clock. "It's three o'clock now. I'll give you a little more than two days' time. Day after tomorrow at seven o'clock in the evening I'll call you and make sure that you've kept your promises."

Suddenly Collin was in a great hurry to leave my grandparents. We were hardly allowed to finish drinking our cocoa.

"After all, we don't have any time to lose," he explained to us when were standing in the street in front of the house.

Since it was still early and a walk after one of Grandma's meals is often the best thing, we decided to go home on foot. Then we could also consider calmly what should be done next. Norbert trotted along beside us, put out again.

"I would love to know if it is Dad's coin. Perhaps we should just ask him," I suggested.

"Under no circumstances!" cried Collin. "That will give everything away. Because if the coin actually belongs to him, then it's also clear that he drew the treasure map."

That wasn't at all clear to me. "Where'd you get that idea?"

"Do you have any other explanation? Why was the coin lying just exactly in front of the cave?"

"And what about the Dinosaurs? Aren't they at all under suspicion anymore? Just think about Nicky's remark!"

"I have. But what I can't figure out is what your father has to do with the Dinosaurs."

"We'll just have to find out," said Steffi.

I could have made that suggestion, too. "And how are we supposed to do that?"

"No idea, brother dear. Perhaps our boss knows?"

He did not know. All the way home we talked over what we should do in the two days we had left to find out what Dad and the Dinosaurs, the cave, the coin, and, of course, the doll and the teddy bear had to do with one another.

"We have to think of something fast, because we don't have much time left," said Collin, as we finally parted. "I do have an idea, but I have to think about it some more in peace and quiet. I'll fill you in on everything tomorrow morning at school."

To our questions about what his idea was, Collin answered with only two words: "Frontal attack!"

False Scents
and a Real Bloodhound

DAD WASN'T THERE AGAIN when we got home. He had another conference.

"How'd it go at Grandpa and Grandma's?" Mom asked when we'd barely got in the door.

"Oh, the same as usual," I answered, hoping she wouldn't ask any more. In vain.

"Were they able to help you with your composition?"

"Oh, yes," Steffi said quickly. "It was very interesting."

"Oh, well, that's good." She grinned as she asked, "Shall I fix you something to eat?"

We said no thank you and quickly went up to our rooms.

Although Collin had told us to think about how

to solve the riddle in two days, there were no brain-storms that evening, at least not for Steffi and me. And the next morning at school we found that it hadn't been any different for Norbert either. That was grist for our boss.

"Well, great! I beat my brains out to get us out of this mess and you don't do anything!"

Finally Steffi broke in. "Then why don't you enlighten us about the idea you had yesterday? And what did you mean by a frontal attack?"

"All right, then, I'll tell you. I meant that we should try to get the ones that are still left on our suspects list to give themselves away."

"Who's left, anyway?" Norbert asked.

"Who else! Mr. Rademacher and the Dinosaurs."

"But my father couldn't have drawn the treasure map," Steffi cut in. "He was still too young for that."

"I didn't say he drew the map. Maybe he only found it before we did. In any case, he's had the coin for a few years already. And it looked like the one that Radish found. So probably he also has some-thing to do with the whole thing."

Of course I feared this, too.

"And what about the Dinosaurs?" Norbert asked again.

Collin made a face. "They've probably been spying on us. They were certainly the ones who took the doll and the teddy bear out of the cave. And they probably mean to snatch our treasure out of our hands, too. But we'll take care of them."

"How?"

"Good question, partner. I had a really stupendous idea. We'll lure the Dinosaurs after a false scent!"

"Cool!" cried Norbert. "How?"

Collin poked his forefinger into Norbert's chest. "Aha! How! That's my stupendous idea! Radish's father made me think of it."

"Our father!" Steffi cried. "What did he have to do with it?"

"Just this: what would your father do to someone who was digging around in his yard?"

Steffi and I were not entirely agreed on whether he would strangle them, hang them, quarter them, or burn them at the stake.

"You see," said Collin, grinning. "I thought so. He got so excited about my stupid shovel."

"So?" I inquired.

"We'll give the Dinosaurs a few tips. We can stand near them at the next break and talk really loud about the treasure so they have to hear us. We'll just change a few details, such as that the treasure is in the Rademachers' yard."

"Dude! Now I get it."

"Miracles still happen. What do you get, Norbert?"

"When the others think there's a treasure buried in Rademachers' yard, they'll come to get it. And then Mr. Rademacher will catch them!"

I began to feel sorry for the poor Dinosaurs already.

"Exactly!" Our boss was beaming. "And because Radish's father is a teacher, he doesn't get home much later than we do. So he'll be right there to catch them. Get it?"

"Sounds good to me," Steffi said.

"Okay," our boss exulted. "So then you know what to do. At the break we stand where those Dinosaur jerks can hear us. We talk about the gold coins in Rademachers' yard long enough so we're sure they've got it."

A real conspiracy! I liked it. I wondered if the suspects, as Collin always called them, would fall for our deception. The first two hours stretched like taffy. It seemed like an eternity to me until the bell rang for break. I kept wondering the whole time whether it really had been the Dinosaurs who had taken the doll and the teddy bear from the cave.

"We have to get Nicky," Collin whispered as we stood around in the schoolyard. "He's the boss and his people do what he says."

Collin probably wanted to subtly indicate to us that we should please follow their example.

Steffi didn't think about that. "How come? It doesn't matter who we tell there's a golden treasure in our yard. If one of them knows, they'll all know. Instead we should pick out the dumbest. We can convince him most easily."

"And who's the dumbest?" Norbert asked.

"They're all dumb. So we'll pick out the super-dumbest."

"Are you talking to yourself?" someone said behind Collin. He turned around. "What?"

"You said 'superdumbest' and I though you were talking about yourself."

It was James. He also belonged to the Dinosaur-Man Gang.

"I was talking about your boss, if you really want to know," Collin shot back.

"I have no boss. And if you mean Nicky, he's our chief."

"Dude! Are you Indians or what?"

James ignored Norbert's remark. "What do you want with him?"

"We don't want anything with him, you moron!" I put it bravely. That's much easier when you belong to a gang yourself.

"Is he one of you now, too?" James asked our boss.

"Sure. You got something against it?"

"Naw. What do I care about your dopey detective stuff? You only took him in anyway because he found the treasure map."

"Oh, so you know about that, do you? You probably heard that from your chief."

"Of course. We don't have any secrets from each other."

"As if anyone cares," said Collin.

"I don't care about your stupid treasure, which doesn't even exist, anyhow."

Before any one of us could answer, James turned around and trotted over to his gang members who were gathered in one corner of the schoolyard.

"Now he's gone," said Norbert. "And we didn't even tell him that the gold is in Radish's yard."

"Then we'll just have to try it again," Steffi said.

"Exactly," Collin agreed. "We'll position ourselves near them and talk loudly but discreetly about the gold."

Steffi waved that away. "That won't do any good. You just saw that."

"But you said yourself—"

"I didn't mean that we should tell it to them."

"What else?"

"We write it for them."

"I don't understand," Norbert said.

"Very simple. We let them find a treasure map. We take a piece of paper and draw a map with a hoard of gold in our yard. Then we let it drop somewhere in their vicinity."

Naturally Collin was enthusiastic. "Cool plan, Steffi. Very frankly, totally cool."

For me there was a still a little snag, however. "Who's supposed to draw the thing?"

"As always, he who asks the dumb question," was Steffi's answer.

"Dude! Why not? You can draw so well. You always have the best grades in art."

"Potato printing is a little different from drawing treasure maps, Norbert. No, no, leave me out of it."

Collin gave me a friendly clap on the shoulder. "Aw, come on, Radish! Be a sport. You really can draw the best of any of us."

I knew it was no use arguing. "Well, okay, but don't you dare complain afterward that it isn't pretty enough or not exact enough or you don't like it for some reason." I tried to get out of it one more time.

"Absolutely not, Radish. You know: one for all and all for one."

I spent the whole third period drawing the stupid map. When I was finally done, I realized to my horror that it looked almost exactly like the other treasure map. Only that the treasure cross was in the middle of our yard. As a precaution, I wrote our address next to it, too.

"I don't know why you acted that way before," Steffi whispered to me when I showed her my artwork. "It really looks almost real."

In the little break between the third and fourth periods, Collin sauntered inconspicuously past Nicky's seat and let the map drop. Probably a little too inconspicuously. Ten minutes before the end of school, my masterpiece was still lying on the floor. We were having English with Big Al. Really his name is Mr. Stevens, but everyone calls him Big Al. It's the perfect name for him. Nobody can say exactly how heavy he is, but the estimates range between a cow and King Kong. When he walks through the classroom and his belly is passing me, Oliver is just seeing his rear end disappear. Oliver sits two rows behind me.

Big Al walked on the map at least three times during his usual wanderings through the classroom. So the beautiful white paper was gradually taking on the color of the floor. The chances that Nicky would ever pick it up were getting slimmer and slimmer. And the end of the hour was coming closer and closer!

It was Norbert, of all people, who had the saving

idea. "Dude," he whispered three times. It took Nicky that long to realize that he was talking to him.

"What do you want?"

"Is that your note lying on the floor?"

Nicky looked at the dirty thing. "No, I don't think so."

Norbert didn't give up. "Look anyhow. Maybe it does belong to you."

Finally Nicky bent over and picked it up. Norbert couldn't really have made it any more obvious. Nicky looked at my drawing for a long time. Then he poked James and the two of them bent over it, whispering.

Steffi gave me a wink. I turned around and saw that Collin was nodding in satisfaction. That had worked just in time. A few minutes later the bell rang and school was out. Before we went home, we agreed to meet in Steffi's room that afternoon.

"Have any of the Dinosaurs showed up yet?" was Collin's first question when I opened the door to him.

"No. Not so far."

"And where's your father?"

"He's puttering around in the yard."

"That's good. Then we can concentrate on our second problem in peace and quiet. But let's go to Steffi's room first."

When we got there, my sister and Norbert were waiting for us. Half the chocolate I'd provided had vanished in the time it had taken me to go to the door to let Collin in.

"Dude!" Norbert greeted us. "I already ate some."

"Don't you have anything else to worry about?" Collin scolded him. "We have to figure out how we can get the treasure out of your neighbor's garden. We only have until tomorrow."

"How do you know the treasure is under the woodpile at all?" Steffi asked suddenly. "The map could always be wrong or someone could have dug it up long ago."

Collin looked at Steffi wide-eyed. "Do you think so?"

"It's possible, isn't it?"

"So?" Collin asked. "What shall we do?"

"Don't know. But before we risk going into Grimm's yard again, I want to know whether the treasure is still there."

"Okay with me. But how?"

"I had an idea about that," Norbert came in.

"What is it?"

"A dog."

"Are you going on about your dog thing again? Man, let it go!"

"Now let him finish what he's saying first, Collin!" said Steffi, coming to poor Norbert's defense.

"We need a dog," Norbert explained to us once again, "so that we could hold the coin under his nose and then he'd have to look for it. I mean, all dogs love to do that. And if this dog ran to the woodpile then and barked, we'd know that the treasure is buried there."

"Man, Norbert! You don't seriously think—" Collin stopped in mid-sentence, stared into the distance for a moment, then jumped up and ran out of the room.

"Dude! What's eating him now?"

Before Steffi or I could say anything, Collin was back with us again. He was waving the scrap of material that I'd found in the cave.

"That's it, partners!"

Steffi tapped her forehead with her index finger. "Are you feeling all right? And just what do you intend to do with that old rag?"

"What do I intend to do with it? Duh! The doll and the teddy bear were sitting on this thing for I don't know how long. If we hold it under the dog's nose, he'll dash right off. You can bet on that!"

"Maybe. Only then he's looking for the doll and the teddy bear and not for the treasure."

"Yeah, yeah, I know. But that's better than nothing. And whoever has the doll and the bear certainly also knows something about the treasure. Then we're at least one step further . . . or do you have a better suggestion?"

We didn't.

But then I had to ask, "And where are we supposed to get a dog?"

"We could borrow one," Steffi suggested.

"Who from?"

"Didn't you say that your next-door neighbor has a dog?" Norbert asked.

"You can forget him," Steffi said. "He wouldn't smell a pig's foot if you held it right under his nose. Besides, he doesn't bark, he coughs, at most. But I just thought of someone we could borrow a dog from."

"Who?" cried Norbert, Collin, and I at the same time.

"Farmer Beckman."

"Does he have a dog?" Norbert asked.

"Absolutely."

Now I couldn't imagine how this was supposed to work. "And you think that Farmer Beckman would lend him to us?"

"Oh well, perhaps not him—actually, it's a her—but I know that his dog has just had puppies.

We could get one of them. They're sure to be terribly sweet."

"And he's supposed to give us one?" I asked again. "Just like that?"

"Man, Radish!" cried Collin. "Don't you understand? We'll get it secretly."

"Of course we'll take it back again afterward," Steffi added.

No kidding. If we showed up at home with a dog I could just picture what our parents would say to us.

"All right, then," Collin declared, "the matter is decided. We go to Farmer Beckman and snatch—I mean, borrow—a dog. Now there's only the question of who should do it."

I had a sinking feeling I already knew.

Operation "Beckman's Dog" and Fat Bertha

BEFORE COLLIN ORGANIZED US for dog snatching, I still had an entirely different problem to solve. I hadn't trusted myself to speak about it before. But now I couldn't ignore it anymore.

"Uh, by the way," I began as inoffensively as possible, "I still have something to take care of."

"So what do you have to take care of?" Collin emphasized the *you* so oddly that at first I didn't want to answer him at all. But then I reminded myself that I did want something from him.

"We have to take someone else with us."

"No!" cried Steffi. "Not the tiny tot!"

"I really don't want to either, but I promised Mrs. Hansen," I admitted. It was true, in fact. Since I'd become a partner in Collin's detective agency I was less and less interested in baby-sitting Bobby. He even got on my nerves. But I wasn't going to let on to that under any circumstances.

Strangely it was Collin, of all people, who came to my rescue. "I don't think it's so bad if the kid comes along. He can even be useful to us."

"He can? How?"

"It's always innocent looking when you have little kids along. After all, we intend to snatch—I mean, borrow—a dog. So the more unsuspicious we are, the better."

"How do you figure that?"

"Because, for example, the little kid can be the pretext for getting Farmer Beckman out of his house."

"How's that supposed to work?" Steffi asked.

"I haven't figured that out precisely yet. But something good will come to me. For instance, we could say that he was hungry and ask Farmer Beckman for a glass of milk."

"That will never work!" cried Steffi. "Farmer Beckman is not stupid."

"How are we supposed to transport the dog, anyhow?" I said, changing the subject. "After all, we can't carry him down the street in our arms."

Collin nodded. "You're right. That would be much too conspicuous."

"The picnic basket!" I cried. "Our old picnic basket is still sitting down in the cellar. It has a lid. I think there's even a lock on it."

Collin thumped me on the shoulder. "Good, Radish. Outstanding. So the problem's solved."

I have to admit that I was pleased with Collin's praise. Really, Collin wasn't so bad. "So that leaves only the question of how we divide up."

"So, what are you thinking?" I asked Collin in the hope that he still hadn't thought about it. I was kidding myself.

"I suggest we do it the way we did last time," Collin continued.

"Last time?" I asked. "Have we ever snatched a dog?"

"No! I mean our Operation 'Witchhunt.' Only then it was you and Steffi who distracted your neighbor, and Norbert and I did the work. For Operation 'Beckman's Dog' we should definitely divide up again."

Norbert nodded. "I think that's a good idea."

"But, of course, this time, we'll divide up differently," declared our boss. I knew it!

"This time I'll undertake the distraction maneuver."

"If you think that I—"

"I didn't say that at all," Collin interrupted my furious sister. "I mean that you and I will undertake the distraction maneuver, while Radish and Norbert—"

"Dude! Why me again?"

"Man, Norbert! Just think about the treasure. A person has to make sacrifices for that. Besides, we'll take the kid along with us, too. He really knows Steffi better than the two of us. Imagine we're standing with Farmer Beckman and the kid begins to scream. Do you know how to calm him down again?"

"Oh, all right, I don't care. I'll do it," Norbert muttered. Picturing himself standing in front of Farmer Beckman with a crying baby in his arms probably convinced him.

"Great!" Collin said happily. "So everything's settled."

I also had no great desire to get the dog. The thought of what would happen if Farmer Beckman caught us filled me with alarm. But I didn't really have any other choice. After all, last time I had undertaken the distraction maneuver, as Collin called it. So I only asked, "How do you intend to distract Farmer Beckman?"

Collin shrugged. "No idea. We have to find some sort of pretext to keep him talking as long as possible. At least long enough so you have time to get the dog. But that certainly won't take long."

"Well, you could say that you have to write a composition for school. A day on the farm or something like that. He'll certainly believe that teachers have ideas like that."

"I'll bet he would believe that," my sister agreed. "After all, we really have had to write compositions like that."

"We certainly have," said Norbert with a sigh.

We'd convinced Collin. "All right, that's okay with me. We'll say that we have to write a composition about a farm."

"But you take the kid!" Steffi cried.

Collin nodded graciously. "Yeah, yeah, sure. Now we just have to be sure that it all works out timewise. The best thing would be if Steffi and I go first. I say we should separate just before we come to the field path. Then give us five minutes. That ought to be enough for the path to the farm."

"And what do we do?" Norbert wanted to know.

"I just told you! You wait five minutes and then come along behind us. Naturally you have to sneak in, best from behind, across the fields.

"Dude! That's all full of mud!"

Norbert was right. The fields behind Farmer Beckman's farm are all swamp.

"Then wear rubber boots," Collin said offhandedly. "Do you have any?" he asked me.

"Sure. They're in the basement."

"And where am I supposed to get mine?" Norbert asked.

"You can wear my father's."

I thought I'd heard wrong. Because Dad is really quite touchy when it comes to his things. "Do you think Dad would allow that?"

"We don't have to ask him, that's all. He who asks many questions receives many answers."

"Exactly!" cried Norbert. "Besides, I'm only going to *wear* the boots, not sell them."

"So let's go down cellar before my father shows up," said Steffi. "And we need the picnic basket too."

When we opened the door to her room, we heard Dad's voice in the kitchen. We took off our shoes and sneaked down the stairs. The rubber boots were standing right next to the cellar stairs. We had to look for a while for the picnic basket. Finally we found it among some junk in the farthest corner of the cellar. My parents hadn't used it for a very long time, so it was very dusty. Plus, the lock didn't work anymore. "We'll take it anyhow," Collin decided. "You'll just have to hold the cover closed so that our Tracker doesn't hop out."

As we sneaked up the cellar stairs again, I heard a strange sound. Since we'd turned out the light as a precaution, I couldn't figure out what it was. It

111

was only when we got out onto the street that Norbert began to lag behind.

"Why are you walking so funny?" I asked him.

"Your father's boots are way too big for me!" he wailed. "Every step I take, I'm afraid I'm going to lose them. I hope I don't get stuck in the mud."

"Quit complaining," Collin said. "Let's just get going. The sooner we begin, the faster we'll have it over with."

"I still have to get Bobby!" I cried. I'd almost forgotten.

Mrs. Hansen had Bobby's things all packed. I only had to put him in his stroller. I quickly ran back up to the next corner. We'd agreed to meet there so my parents couldn't see us.

I pushed the stroller up to Collin's feet. "Here, you wanted to push him."

Collin took him without protesting. We went up to the field path that led to Farmer Beckman's farm.

Collin stopped. "So, here we separate. You wait five minutes, as we discussed. Everything clear?"

We nodded and he went off pushing Bobby. Somehow the three of them looked like father, mother, and child. It was weird.

They were scarcely out of hearing when Norbert pulled on my sleeve. "Dude! Come on, we'll go too."

"But Collin just said—"

"It doesn't matter what he said. I can hardly walk in these stupid rubber boots. If we wait any longer, Collin and Steffi will be back here before we've gotten to the farmyard."

He was right. On Norbert's short legs the rubber boots looked even more gigantic. It would actually be better if we went now. I took the picnic basket, or we wouldn't have been able to make any progress at all.

The field was almost entirely mud. We sank into the ground with every step. When we pulled our boots out there was a loud, smacking sound.

Finally we reached the barnyard. We had seen and heard nothing more of Steffi, Bobby, and Collin since we started out. Fortunately, there was no sign of Farmer Beckman either. If I even thought about the possibility of his catching us, my stomach turned over. The way he looked, he wasn't to be fooled around with.

I turned around to Norbert. "Everything okay?"

He was snorting like a locomotive. "Let's get it over with."

We looked around for the dog kennel. We were lucky. It was between two sheds, so that it couldn't be seen from the entrance to the farmhouse. But with that our luck came to an end. We were only a few yards away from the kennel —I could already see the puppies—when something black shot out at us. Norbert and I both saw it at the same time and ran like mad. We stormed up to the door of one of the sheds. It wasn't locked, so we sprang inside in one leap and I slammed the door behind us.

My heart was in my throat. When I'd calmed down a little, I peeked through a little hole in the door. Farmer Beckman's dog was standing in front of the shed, barking and growling her head off. Luckily she was chained. She was almost as big as we were and if the chain had been only a little longer, she would probably have eaten us: picnic basket, rubber boots, and all.

"What do we do now?" Norbert whispered. "I could see the puppies. They were lying in the kennel."

"You can go get one," I whispered back.

"Are you nuts? I want to live."

"Right. Let's just get out of here fast. Who knows if a chain like that can snap."

"Dude! How do you intend to get out of here? That monster is standing right in front of the door!"

I looked around me in the dim light. Only now did I realize where we were: in the chicken coop! Actually, it was more like an open area with dozens of feathered creatures strutting around cheerfully. Farmer Beckman must've been some kind of environmentally conscious farmer. Now I understood the sign on the road: BECKMAN'S FRESH COUNTRY EGGS FROM HAPPY CHICKENS!

Farmer Beckman's happy chickens were running all over our feet, scratching and pecking around on the ground and cackling back and forth. Sometimes I thought that one or the other of them was eyeing us mistrustfully. But I might have been mistaken.

"Maybe there's another way out of here," I whispered to Norbert.

I looked around and then I saw a back entrance. We were saved!

Suddenly Norbert grabbed my sleeve. "What're we going to say to Collin?"

"What else should we say? We tell him what happened."

"And if he doesn't believe us?"

"Do you mean that he'd think . . ."

". . . that we were cowards," Norbert finished. He was right. As well as I had gotten to know Collin, he would at least be suspicious. Without the coin and the old rag he would never even have believed me about the doll and the teddy bear.

"Do you have any idea what we could do?" I asked Norbert. "No way I'm passing by that dog."

"Me either. But we need some kind of proof that we were here."

"Well said. But what?"

"Dude! Let's take a chicken!"

"Are you insane? What are we supposed to do with a chicken?"

"How do I know. Maybe it will work with a chicken as well as a dog. Anyhow, we just need something to show Collin. Besides, he'll do anything anyhow, as long as he's allowed to be the boss. The main thing is that we can prove we were here."

Of course it was a harebrained idea, but we had no other choice. When I thought about Collin, a chicken was still better than an empty picnic basket.

But first we had to catch one! We had no time to lose. Who knew how long Collin and Steffi could hold Farmer Beckman. If he hadn't already gotten suspicious ages ago with all the racket.

Quickly and firmly I pressed the basket into Norbert's hands, took a deep breath, and made a grab for one of the cacklers that was eating. It wasn't so easy. They all looked the same. Finally I discovered one that was a little fatter than the others. I hoped that would mean she couldn't move so fast. Secretly I dubbed her Bertha, so I could distinguish her even better from the others. I sneaked up to about three feet from her. My victim was calmly pecking around on the ground, oblivious to my stalking. With one leap, which would have done honor to a panther, I sprang soundlessly at Bertha, the unsuspecting—and landed in a big heap of chicken manure. The stupid creature had cried "Buck, buck!" just before my landing and done a little hop to the side.

When I got over my first shock, I saw that she was working over the floor again. My attack hadn't impressed her in the least. I stood very quietly, wiping chicken manure off my trousers. What I needed was a plan. After all, I had more brains in my head than the whole chicken society put together. Norbert would have to help me.

"Watch out," I whispered to him without taking my eyes off my quarry. "Put the basket on the floor and open the cover. When we have the chicken, it all has to go very fast."

Norbert nodded. "Got it. Catch chicken, into basket, close cover, and vamoose."

"Exactly. Now, you stand over in back in the corner. See that hen there?" I pointed at Fat Bertha.

"The one with the white spot on her rear end?"

"Yeah. Her name's Bertha. Okay?"

"How do you know her name's Bertha. You know her?"

"Shut up! I just named her Bertha. So I can tell her from the others better."

"Oh, okay," was all Norbert said.

"I'm going to go for Bertha. If she gets away from me, she'll probably flutter in your direction. Then you have to chase her back again so I can try it again."

I would rather not go into detail about what happened next. I only remember it very hazily anyhow. In any case, it was even more difficult than I had imagined. How often I landed between the hens in manure I don't really remember. Only that I got madder and madder and the chickens got louder and louder. In the end I could hardly see my hand in front of my face for all the noisy, cackling confusion of chickens, feathers, and acrid white dust. Meanwhile Norbert and I were leaping around like idiots, and outside the door Farmer Beckman's mother dog was barking her head off.

Somehow Norbert managed to shout through the deafening noise. "It's no use! We're making too much noise! The farmer is sure to come now!"

As he spoke he waved his arms wildly. Our uncooperative fat lady hadn't planned for that. She was trying to fly past Norbert quite close, probably to graze him and make him mad. In any case, he caught her right in one of his arm swings. It looked as though he'd made a volleyball serve. Bertha sailed past my head and landed in the vicinity of the picnic basket. Norbert must have hit her in a key spot. She kept herself on her feet, certainly, but she staggered around and waggled her head. A chance like this would never come again! Not that I want to boast, but at that moment I was totally clear-headed. I was next to her in one leap, then I grabbed her by the throat and stuffed her into the basket. She was making a strange gurgling sound.

"Dude!" shrieked Norbert over the racket, although he was standing right next to me. "You've killed her!"

I picked up the basket and held it against my ear. I was awfully glad when I clearly heard a soft "Buck, buck."

"She's still alive," I reassured Norbert.

"Well, thank goodness. Now let's get out of here!"

Luckily the back door wasn't locked either. There was no longer any question of a careful retreat as we'd once planned. To be precise, we ran away from there as fast as we could. That was Norbert's fault. Just as we came out of the coop, he suddenly yelled in my ear so that I almost died of fright, "The farmer's coming! The farmer's coming! I just saw him!"

I had no more time to turn around to see if he was right because he ran off as if he'd been stung by hornets. I thought about Farmer Beckman's steam-shovel hands and ran like the wind behind him. I caught up with him after a few yards and passed him, even though I was carrying Fat Bertha. Mud splashed into my face, but it didn't bother me, any more than Norbert's wailing behind me. He kept calling something to me. But I couldn't exactly understand him. I was much too busy myself. Besides, Fat Bertha was making an infernal commotion. I only heard every now and then that it had something to do with boots.

I didn't stop and look around me until I'd reached the sanctuary of the street corner. There was nothing to be seen of Farmer Beckman. Meanwhile Bertha had also grown quiet. She was probably too exhausted to cackle. Then Norbert limped up, protesting. His face was beet-red.

"Dude, you goofball!" he panted at me. "Couldn't you wait? I was calling to you the entire time back there."

"I know, but you can just tell me about it now, can't you?"

"Could someone perhaps reveal to me which steamroller you two went under?"

Collin had Bobby in his arms. Steffi was standing right next to him. They still looked like a family. I had no idea how long they'd been waiting for us when I came running up. I hadn't noticed them.

"You look hilarious!" cried Steffi, before I could answer Collin.

I looked at Norbert. He looked awful. Though what I could see of myself wasn't much better. He was covered with filth from head to foot, with the white dust the chicken coop and the black from the field. Everything was full of it: his hair, his face, his jacket, his hands, his trousers and the rubber—

"Where's the other boot?" I screamed at him.

"That's what I was trying to tell you the whole time! But you wouldn't listen!" he screamed back. "The stupid rubber boot is stuck in the mud back there!"

"Where?"

"Right behind the chicken coop. And because I was afraid Farmer Beckman was after us I didn't dare run back and get it."

"You'll do that right now, Norbert," said Steffi coolly. "If my father notices that we've lost his boot, we're in big trouble."

"Now?" screamed Norbert even louder. "Have you fallen on your head? Have you got any idea what we've been through? Ten horses couldn't drag me back there again!"

"Hey, what stinks?" Collin broke in on the two squabblers. He came over to me and started sniffing around.

Bobby sniffed too and made a face.

"Man, you stink something awful!"

"Now, will you finally tell us what happened? Do you have the dog?" cried Steffi breaking into Collin's completely uncalled-for attack of laughter.

"You tell first," said Norbert.

That was good. That would give us more time.

"Oh, it really wasn't so hard," said Steffi. "Of course we had to look for Farmer Beckman for a little while, but then we found him—in the pigsty."

"Oh, man," Collin interrupted. "Have you any idea how bad that stinks?"

"Compared to that, you guys smell like roses," Steffi said with a grin.

I ignored these remarks. "And?"

"At first he was very suspicious," my sister continued. "He didn't want to talk with us. He had too much to do, he said."

"Finally we did it, though," Collin went on. "I had to use my very best arts of persuasion, believe you me. Then we filled him in on the supposed school composition. We wanted to get him to tell us something about the life on the farm. That would certainly have kept him busy for a good long time."

"Did he?" I asked.

"No, he didn't," Steffi replied. "He just kept saying that he had much too much to do and that we should come back another day."

122

"And then the whole thing got a lot hairier."

"How come?"

"Because we were hearing strange noises from outside. Anyhow, Farmer Beckman kept going to the door and murmuring, 'Something's not right out there.' We couldn't exactly hear what. The pigs had just been fed. Man, what a grunting and smacking. Disgusting!"

Norbert and I exchanged meaningful glances.

"We were thinking that it had something to do with you," Steffi continued. "We talked to him like crazy. We almost talked his ear off. But I had the feeling that the commotion was getting worse and there was no end to it. But I probably only imagined that because I was so nervous."

Again Norbert and I exchanged looks.

"But suddenly it stopped," said Collin. "There wasn't a peep to be heard outside. And then we got out of there. Otherwise Farmer Beckman would probably have thrown us out. Of course we hoped that you'd had enough time to get the dog."

"Did you?" asked Steffi. "Is the dog in there?"

"Yes, uh," said Norbert. "Actually . . ."

"What's the matter?" cried Collin "Did you or didn't you?"

"Not exactly," I answered diplomatically.

"Give it here!" Collin screamed at me. Before I

could defend myself, he snatched the basket out of my hand.

He slammed open the lid, looked inside, and immediately slammed it shut again. He said nothing, only stared at the basket.

"What's the matter?" Steffi asked finally. "Is the dog in there? Let's see!"

"Do you know what these two have done?" screamed Collin, so loud that his voice broke. "They snatched a chicken! Can't you idiots tell the difference between a dog and a chicken? A chicken goes *buck-buck* and a dog goes *woof-woof*!"

It took a while to tell what happened because Steffi was laughing so hard she almost wet her pants.

"And what now?" Steffi asked when we were finished and she was wiping the tears out of her eyes.

Collin shrugged his shoulders. "I can't imagine that it works with chickens the way it does with dogs."

"Dude! Let's at least try, anyhow. If we don't try, we'll never know. But you're the boss and you have to decide about it."

Collin took a deep breath. "Okay, it's all right with me. But if it doesn't work, you'll take the critter back and get the dog."

Saying that, he turned around and pushed off with Bobby's stroller and Fat Bertha under his arm.

"We'll just see about that!" Norbert yelled and hobbled along behind him in one boot. As he did so, he looked over at me and winked. Luckily Steffi didn't see it.

When we caught up with the two of them, our boss was again forging plans.

"We have no time to lose," he said. "So we'll have to try it now."

"And where?" I wanted to know, although I really didn't care. I've never heard of a hen that could track anything.

"The best would naturally be the cave. But we'd have to pass the farm to get there. And that seems to me too dangerous at the moment."

My thoughts exactly.

"So we'll try it first in the vicinity of the wood-pile at the back of your neighbor's garden."

"And if old lady Grimm sees us?"

"We'll have to take that risk. And if it doesn't work with the hen, we'll have to come up with something else. Besides, we can sneak in from behind."

We did. We got to the far side of Miss Grimm's garden without any more incidents. We knelt around the basket with Fat Bertha inside it.

"So," whispered Collin. "Who's going to take her out?"

"Radish," said Norbert at once. "He caught her."

"Do I have to?" I defended myself feebly.

But Collin was merciless. "Go on and do it. If Norbert won't do it, you're the only one left. After all, Steffi and I don't want to smell like chicken poop, too."

Up until that moment Bertha had been strangely quiet. I was afraid that she'd departed this life. But that was a mistake. She was only waiting for the right moment. And it came when I lifted the lid. I never knew that chickens could make such a racket. I immediately clapped the lid shut again. But it didn't help. Her cackling resounded like an alarm siren. That's probably why we didn't notice the menace that was creeping up on soft soles.

Miss Grimm's New Children

SOMETHING THAT WEIGHED AT LEAST A TON fell on my shoulder. Now I knew the meaning of that line we had recently read in the Bible in Sunday school: "And God's powerful voice rent the earth and made the heavens tremble." A voice like that was thundering so in my ear that my eardrum almost burst: "I finally caught you!"

It was Farmer Beckman. Because we were kneeling, he looked even more gigantic than he actually is. One hand was still clamped onto my shoulder, and with the other he was waving Dad's rubber boot like a club.

"Drive my chickens crazy and then on top of it swipe my best layer!" he scolded in his thundering voice. "You dratted bunch of rascals!"

As far as I was concerned, the dratted bunch of rascals had buzzing in the head, stomach gripes, abdominal cramps, and shaking knees all at the same time. Nevertheless, I was glad that Dad's boot was back. He really is so touchy when it comes to his things.

I stood up. Farmer Beckman shrank a little. A very little. "Could I please have the boot, Mr. Beckman? You see, it belongs to my father."

"Your father?" He squeezed my shoulder so that my bones crunched. "So you're that kind of a family, are you? The head thief teaches his tricks to the young, eh?"

"It wasn't like that at all!" said Norbert, trying to clear up the error. "I had actually borrowed—"

"Poppycock! Excuses won't do you any good anymore. I'll tell him a thing or two, your fine father!"

I had to keep him from going to Dad. I wanted to say something, to clear up the whole thing. I couldn't do it. Something was squeezing my throat shut. My mouth was as dry as if I'd been wandering in the desert for a week.

Luckily there was someone else there who knew Dad well. "No!" cried Steffi. "Not my father! We'll make it up to you. For instance, we could clean out the pigsty!"

"Dude! Are you nuts? I thought you said it stank?"

"None of that! I'm going to have a serious talk with your father. After all, we're not in the Wild West here."

I wasn't so sure about that.

"Hello!" he bellowed into Grimm's yard. "Is anyone there? Come out! I have your fine little troublemakers here! And I'm not leaving here until you personally come and get them!"

"What's all that noise about?" croaked a voice on the other side of the hedge.

"Oh, no! The witch!" moaned Collin, who until that moment had been kneeling there on the ground as motionless as an altar boy. Something was moving behind the hedge and a few branches were spread apart. Between them Miss Grimm's face appeared. She had a fire-engine-red bandana with white polka dots on her head and a broom in her hand. All that was missing was a black cat on her shoulder.

"What in heaven's name is going on here?" she screeched. She looked at Steffi and me, "Ah, it's you. I might have known. Whenever there's any racket going on, you're not far away."

"Now listen to me for a moment, madam!" thundered Farmer Beckman, cutting her off. "Do

129

you know what your children have done? And your husband helped them do it."

"Children? Husband? Now you listen to me, mister. I have no husband. And so of course I have no children. And of that I am very glad, understand?"

"Well, well, so you have no children. And who, if you please, are these here? Are they perhaps spirits?"

Farmer Beckman held Dad's boot up high. "And what is this here? Is it not perhaps your husband's boot?"

"Are you accusing me of lying?" Miss Grimm swung her broom threateningly.

"Yes indeed, that's what I'm doing! You only want to dodge having to answer for what your brood has done!" Farmer Beckman swung the boot threateningly.

"My brood? What impertinence!"

"Yes indeed. Your brood! And an impertinence most certainly!"

Miss Grimm and Farmer Beckman got louder and louder. Thinking we were Miss Grimm's children was such an insult. So Steffi, Collin, Norbert, and I tried to scream against the two of them to clear up the mistake. Miss Grimm screeched, Farmer Beckman bellowed, and we screamed in between. On top of it all, Bobby began to howl and Fat Bertha was cackling as if her basket were on fire. To sum up, it was a tremendous commotion. And of course, it wasn't without consequences. Suddenly I saw my father bending over the low fence that he'd spent the whole Easter vacation installing.

"What's going on here?"

Although he hadn't called very loudly, it was immediately as quiet as a graveyard. Even Bobby stopped howling.

"Is that your husband?" Farmer Beckman screamed at Miss Grimm. In one great step, Dad climbed over the fence.

"Austin! Stefanie! What's going on here?"

"Hi, Dad," I said. "Mr. Beckman and Miss Grimm, I mean Norbert and I, uh . . ."

"Isn't that my boot?" He interrupted my stammering. "And what in heaven's name happened to you?"

"Obviously it's your boot!" cried Farmer Beckman. "That's why I'm here, after all."

"Well, that's very nice of you. Many thanks."

"What's many thanks got to do with all this? After all, you lost it in my field when you—"

"Now, this business is beginning to be too silly for me," Dad broke in. "Could you please give me my boot? I would like to work in my garden."

"You want the boot, do you? Oh no, mister! You won't get it. It's a piece of evidence!"

"My boot?"

"Dude!" screamed Norbert so angrily in the midst of all this that Farmer Beckman finally listened to him.

"Mr. Rademacher had absolutely nothing to do with it!" Norbert was like one possessed. "I only borrowed the boots because I didn't have any and because the whole meadow was full of mud, but they were much too big for me, and then when we were running away with Fat Bertha, because I thought that you had discovered us, one of them got stuck in the mud, but I didn't dare turn around again because we had to take Fat Bertha because the dog growled at us and because I thought that you would be really angry at us and that was right, too, because here you are and you are really, really angry!"

Farmer Beckman stood there like a statue. He stared at Norbert with an open mouth. Norbert would certainly have kept on babbling, only he couldn't because he had to take a breath. "Does that mean that your father has nothing at all to do with the affair?"

"That's what we've been trying to explain to you the whole time!" cried Collin, finally speaking up.

I was surprised that Farmer Beckman blushed. I

would not have expected that of him.

"I am really very sorry. I suspected you and your husband completely unjustly. I beg your pardon a thousand times," he said quietly to Miss Grimm.

He still didn't understand that she wasn't our mother. Why, for Pete's sake, do grown-ups never listen to us? Steffi and I looked at each other. She shook her head. She was right. Why go to the trouble when it was pointless?

"Oh, no!" cried Collin suddenly. "Not them too!"

At the same moment I saw two grinning faces come around the corner. They belonged to the Dinosaurs, Nicky and James, to be more specific.

"What are you doing here?" Steffi yelled at them.

They didn't have to answer. Collin knew it already. "It's obvious! They intend to dig up the treasure!"

"Treasure!" Nicky bellowed back. "What a load of . . . There isn't any treasure at all!"

"Oh, really? Then you probably also want us to believe that you didn't swipe the doll and teddy bear out of the cave, right?"

The Dinosaurs stopped at a safe distance.

"Doll? Teddy bear? What's that supposed to mean? Is that another one of your tricks? We only wanted to know why you wanted to lead us here with the false treasure map." He held up the map that I'd drawn in school.

"How do you know it's false?" Steffi asked him.

James grinned. "Because." He turned the map over. I immediately knew what he meant. I'd drawn the map on my new Batman drawing paper!

I squinted over toward Collin as meekly as possible. He didn't say anything. But he looked as if he were just about to have a nervous breakdown.

Of course the grown-ups didn't have the slightest idea of what was going on now. Even Miss Grimm was speechless. And Farmer Beckman was completely confused.

"Are these your children, too?" he asked Miss Grimm politely. She'd given up. She simply nodded.

"What is going on here, anyway?" Dad broke in. I could see lots of red spots on his neck. "What were my rubber boots doing in Mr. Beckman's meadow? And who is Fat Bertha?"

"The hen that we borrowed from Mr. Beckman," Norbert explained.

"What?"

"They stole a hen from me, you see," Farmer Beckman explained to my father. "My best layer, at that."

"What? I mean, we will of course compensate you for any damages."

"No, no, not necessary. Nothing happened. Just give me back the hen and then we'll forget the whole thing."

Probably Farmer Beckman must have felt guilty for accusing Dad to let us off so easily.

"Where is this hen?" Dad wanted to know.

I pointed to our old picnic basket. "In there."

Farmer Beckman bent over, opened the cover, and pulled Bertha out with one grab. I would have loved to ask him how he did that.

He smiled lovingly at Fat Bertha. "Now everything will be all right and we can go home."

"Can't we do anything else for you?" Dad asked him. "After all, you've had considerable inconvenience because of the children."

"Already forgotten. Just keep a better eye on them in the future."

"You can rely on that."

Dad's tone when he said that gave me an idea that we still had more in store for us.

Farmer Beckman had only gone a few steps when he turned around once again. "Perhaps your children could do something for me after all," he said with a sly grin. "Your daughter suggested before that she'd muck out my pigsty. Now that I think about it, I'd like to take her up on the offer."

"All right," replied Dad, grinning just as slyly.

"When should they come?"

"Saturday would be all right with me."

"What time?"

"Let them get their sleep. If they begin at seven o'clock in the morning, that's early enough."

Dad nodded cordially at Farmer Beckman. "All right, I'll see to it that they're at your place punctually. Good-bye, Mr. Beckman."

"Good-bye!"

I always wanted to know how it felt when a person fainted. If Mrs. Hansen hadn't come just then, I probably would have found out that day.

She stormed right up to Bobby, who'd been amusing himself with our picnic basket. Because of the excitement about Bertha nobody had been watching him. Too bad.

Bertha must have felt at home in our basket, because she'd laid an egg. Bobby had found it and was playing with it—that is, he had mixed its contents with sand and stirred up a nice glop. Then he had covered himself with it from head to toe.

"Look at you!" Mrs. Hansen screamed when she saw the mess.

Bobby appeared to feel just fine. He beamed at his mom. She picked him up and looked angrily over at me. I was beginning to get used to being looked at like that.

"Really, Austin, I always thought you were watching him when you were together, but apparently that's not so. Do you have any idea how much work it is to give him a bath? In the future, I'll have to think very carefully about whether I'll hand him over to you again!"

She put Bobby in his stroller and wheeled him away without another glance. On the other hand, Dad just looked at me. He didn't say anything, just shook his head.

Miss Grimm hadn't butted in again since Dad had climbed over the fence. She'd watched the whole performance with great interest. Only once, when Dad and Farmer Beckman agreed that we had to muck out the pigsty, she'd smiled fleetingly. She'd probably be telling the whole neighborhood about it next day. Maybe it would even be in the newspaper.

Only when Mrs. Hansen had disappeared and she knew the show was over, did she deliver her inevitable commentary. "I've always said so. There's something not right about your children, Mr. Rademacher. Not only do they make noise, now they're stealing, too. My God! Just where's this going to lead?"

I don't know what triggered it, but I could see a jolt go through Dad. "My dear Miss Grimm," he said in a dangerously soft voice, "my children did not steal. They said they only borrowed the hen, and I believe them. And as for the noise, I can only say one thing to you: It so happens that they are children. And sometimes children make noise. If you don't like it, you can always move. I would recommend a nice sanitorium for you. If that still isn't quiet enough for you, you can always buy a trailer and park it in the cemetery. You're sure to have your peace and quiet there."

He paused briefly and then he shouted, louder than I had ever heard him, "And now, I never want to hear anything more about it again! Do you understand?"

While Dad was speaking to her, her eyes got bigger and bigger and her jaw dropped lower and lower. Even after he'd stopped talking, she stood there motionless for about a minute, staring at him with her red kerchief on her head and the broom in her hand. Then she took a deep breath, turned on her heel, and was gone. A few seconds later we heard her terrace door slam.

I was about to thank Dad and tell him how terrific I thought it was that he had finally told the old witch what he thought of her, but one look at his face was enough to know that we were next.

"So, fans. Now I want to know what was going

on here. I want to hear the whole story, understand?"

"Whoa, it's so late!" cried Collin. "I have to get
home. My parents are probably wondering where I
am."

Norbert wasn't any braver. "Me, too, Mr.
Rademacher. My mom is wondering where I am,
too."

Those cowards!

But Dad didn't soften. "Five more minutes
won't matter. We'll go into our yard now, where
you can tell me everything. Then you can go home."

"Can we come too?" James and Nicky cried at the
same time. Naturally they didn't want to miss this.

"Do those two have anything to do with it?" Dad
asked me. I just shook my head. There was no point
in trying to explain anything to him.

"Then go home!" he called to the other two.
"Your parents are probably wondering where you
are!"

They hesitated a moment, but then they
stomped off. Nicky turned around once with a huge
grin on his face. "Okay, see you in school tomorrow!"

Collin watched him go. I would have given anything to know what he was thinking at that
moment.

When the Dinosaurs were gone, all four of us ran behind Dad to our yard. Naturally we weren't allowed to climb over the little fence, so we went around the outside.

I kept hoping Mom would see us and come to our rescue. No such luck. We gathered around our patio table. There weren't enough chairs there so Steffi and I sat crosswise on a lounge chair.

"Well," Dad said, looking at us. Really he didn't look angry at all, just kind of curious. "Now, what's the story with this hen that you supposedly only borrowed?"

It took a while before we began to talk because no one wanted to start. But then, when we finally got started, it poured out of us like a waterfall. To be precise, it was Steffi, Collin, and especially Norbert who told Dad everything. I held myself way back. Because I was afraid they were going to find out my own little secret. It was kind of a premonition, and sometimes those can be right.

Secrets and Confessions

DAD LISTENED WITHOUT INTERRUPTING us once. Only his facial expressions changed: curious at first, then amazed, and finally thoughtful.

". . . and just at the moment when Radish was about to take Fat Bertha out of the basket, Mr. Beckman came," Norbert was closing our report. "And you know the rest."

"And he thought that old lady Grimm was our mother," Steffi added, grinning.

Dad looked severely at Steffi. "To you she's always *Miss* Grimm, Stefanie. I must admit, however, that *that* mistake doesn't flatter me particularly."

"And the treasure is still buried in her yard, of all places!" cried Norbert.

Dad scratched his chin and looked at me. "Can you please show me this coin, Austin?"

I don't know if I blushed. Anyway, I was very hot as I rooted around in my wallet for the coin. When I finally had it in my hand, something in me resisted giving it to my dad. But he just kept holding his open hand right under my nose.

"Please, Austin!"

I gave it to him. He cast only a brief glance at it and then looked at me again.

"So that's the treasure coin," he said, utterly calm. But this very calmness made me nervous.

He took the gold coin between thumb and forefinger. "Unfortunately I have to tell you that the coin belongs to me, Austin."

"So, it does," murmured Collin.

"I beg your pardon?"

"Oh, nothing. Never mind, Mr. Rademacher. How do you know that it's your coin?"

"My wife gave it to me for our tenth wedding anniversary. I recognized it by the letter that's scratched into it. It was there when I received it. I'd discovered it in an antique store one time and I really liked it. So my wife got it for me—for our anniversary. I'm really glad to have it back.

"Where did you find it?"

"In the forest."

"In front of a cave!" Norbert added.

"And the treasure map?" Collin asked. "What about the treasure map?"

"That would certainly interest me, too, Austin."

Done for. I'd lost. It was pointless to lie now. I didn't dare look at Dad or the others. But they were all looking at me.

"It wasn't all just a fake, was it?" Steffi cried. "Were you just fooling us the whole time?"

"No, only . . ."

"Only what?"

"Only the map, which . . . which I drew myself."

It was out. I'd said it. I looked at the ground and waited for the sky to fall. But it didn't.

"But why did the map look so old?" was all Norbert asked. He looked like a little boy who's just been told there is no Easter bunny.

"I took the paper from some that was lying around on my closet floor. It was already all yellow."

"Dude! Why did you do that? I don't get it!"

I would gladly have explained everything to just Norbert because he had the least to do with it. But he wouldn't have understood, any more than Collin, Dad, or Steffi would have.

At first I had just wanted to play a trick on them because I was so sick of Collin's attitude. When I discovered the cave, I got the idea about the treasure map only because Collin and Steffi were playing that dumb treasure-seeker game without me. If an old doll and a teddy bear had been sitting there in the cave, why not a treasure map too? Steffi, Collin, and Norbert had believed me right off, too. I only meant to pretend a little and maybe get to be the leader of a treasure hunt. I'd put the treasure in Miss Grimm's yard because I was sure that none of us would dare go in there. But then when we found the coin in front of the cave, I almost believed in the treasure myself. Unfortunately Collin and the others were braver than I'd figured. But I hadn't wanted to tell them the truth, either. I liked being a detective too much. So I simply went along and hoped they'd give up without ever discovering the hoax.

Collin was the first to pull himself together. He jumped up. "It was all a scam!" he yelled. "The coin, the map, the teddy bear, the doll, everything!"

"No!" I yelled back. "The doll and the bear were really there, honest!"

"And we're supposed to believe that?" Steffi asked. "After you lied to us like that?"

So she was mad at me too. What's that saying? Lie once, forever a liar. Normally I find grown-up sayings like that dumb. But there did seem to be some truth to this one.

Collin took Steffi's hand and pulled her up off the lounge chair. "Come on, let's go. I don't want to have anything more to do with him. You, too, Norbert!"

Steffi and Norbert actually stood up.

"From now on you're not a partner anymore! Understand?" Collin yelled at me, turned, and stomped angrily away.

At first I'd been afraid, then I was ashamed, but suddenly I felt something entirely different. I felt a prickling in my stomach region. It kept getting stronger and hotter until I was simply furious. So furious that it didn't matter at all to me what I said. I jumped up and ran after them.

"Just who do you think you are!" I yelled at them. "You can take your dumb detective agency and stick it!"

Collin turned around. "Yeah?" he sneered. "And why were you so anxious to be taken in then?"

"Me? Who asked me to join? It was you. And who wanted to get the reward? You!"

"That's all your fault. If you hadn't lied like that—"

"Do you know what you are?" I interrupted him. I wanted to scream at him, but I was so angry that only a squeak came out. "You're a hypocritical idiot. Yes, that's exactly what you are! All of you."

"Dude! Why us too?"

"Because you all would have done anything just to get the treasure."

"If anyone here is an idiot, it's you!" Collin yelled back.

If Dad hadn't given Miss Grimm a piece of his mind, she would certainly have come over long since and complained that we were making so much noise. But that wouldn't have bothered me in the slightest at that moment.

"Who wanted to interrogate suspicious people? And who kept on making plan after plan? And who acted like a cross between Daniel Boone and James Bond? You, Collin! You even believed that a hen could track, you dope! And now you're making yourself out to be the big boss again! Some boss! You know what I think? I think you're all too dumb to think up such a good idea, and as far as I'm concerned you can all go jump in the lake!"

I turned around and just left them standing there. Of course, I couldn't tell exactly, but I'm pretty sure they all just stared after me in shock. After all, it doesn't happen every day that I have an attack of rage. Without looking around once I ran back to our patio. I dropped onto a chair with trembling knees.

"And you?" Collin suddenly yelled out to me.

146

"What do you do? You run around the neighborhood with babies because you don't have any friends!"

Dad was still sitting in his chair. He hadn't said another word since I'd admitted that I was the treasure-map forger.

"You really gave them what for," he said now.

"Mmm."

"It was right, Austin. Everything you said was right."

"Honest?"

"Yes."

"Do you at least believe me that there really was a doll and a bear?"

"I not only believe you, I know it's true."

"How?"

"Because the doll and the teddy bear belong to me. To be frank, I'm glad that we're alone now, so I can tell you."

I'd thought that nothing more could surprise me today. "They belong to you, Dad? But why, I mean how—"

"I think it's time I told you something, Austin," he interrupted me. "But before I tell you about the doll and the teddy bear, I'd like you to answer a question for me. Did you invent the whole thing with the treasure because you wanted to be taken into this detective gang?"

"Yes, I guess so," I said, though that wasn't it entirely. I just didn't feel like explaining everything to him right then. Besides, I was too curious about what he had to do with the cave in the forest.

He nodded. "I thought so."

"Why?"

"Because it was so much like me. Actually, you remind me a lot of me when I was your age."

"Really? I didn't know that."

"It's true. I wasn't particularly strong either and I avoided sports like the plague. Especially because the others always teased me about it."

"So what did you do?"

"As time went on I kept withdrawing from the others more and more, just like you. Before I knew it, I was a real loner."

I don't think that I'm a loner. I think I get along quite well with most people. I mean, just because I don't have anyone to bring home from school to hang out, I'm still a long way from being a loner, aren't I? But I didn't say anything and let my father talk on. I wondered if maybe he'd also been a baby-sitter when he needed money for comics in those days.

"I didn't of course seek out a small child I could watch as compensation"—guess not—"but I did something else instead."

"What was that?"

"I went into the forest and played there alone. Sometimes in that cave. I had a doll hidden there."

"And a teddy bear," I added.

"Precisely."

"Why were they still in the cave, then, when I found them? Do you still play with them?"

"No!" said Dad, laughing. "You don't have to look so horrified. In time my relationship with my schoolmates changed. I discovered something, you see."

"A secret?"

"No, not a secret. I discovered that I had a special talent—for math."

"Huh?"

He laughed again. "You've already realized that the mathematics you learn in school gets more and more complicated."

Who was he talking to? Of course I knew that.

"All my classmates moaned and groaned about mathematics in those days," Dad continued. "But it didn't give me any trouble at all. I didn't ever have to do much studying for it. I understood it without trying. When I first realized that, I was seized with ambition. I wanted to become absolutely the best in the class in math."

"Did you get to be?" I asked, though I thought I already knew the answer.

"Yes, I did, without any difficulty."

"But what does all that have to do with the doll, the teddy bear, and the cave?"

"Well, it had been a long time since I'd been back to play with them because I was with my classmates more and more often. Besides, we moved just about that time. Grandma and Grandpa thought that was why I had made more friends, and I let them believe that. So when we moved, I didn't take the doll and the bear with me. I just left them there in the cave.

"But when you told me that you'd found the cave, I suddenly began to feel ashamed of myself. Maybe I was just afraid that you would become the way I was in those days. Anyhow, to make a long story short, I decided to get the doll and the bear from the cave . . . I didn't think you'd notice. After all, you'd promised me not to go there again," he added with a meaningful look.

"So then it was you that took the doll and the bear out of the cave."

"Correct."

"And where are they now?"

"Oh, well . . . I . . . I threw them away because I thought that this chapter should finally be closed for good."

Thrown away! Was I supposed to believe that? He'd probably put them in the little cupboard in his study, along with Mom's old love letters to him.

"And so it was you that dropped the coin there?" was all I asked him.

Dad scratched his chin again. "You know, I've been thinking about that the whole time. I only found out from you that I lost it there. But now I think I know how it happened."

"How?"

"There are some big rocks lying in front of the cave. I don't know how often I stumbled over them as a boy. I've already said, sports aren't my thing. That day, when I visited my old cave, it happened again. I sprawled out, headlong. The coin must have fallen out of the little side pocket in my pipe pouch. I always keep it there. When I picked myself up again, I noticed the pouch lying open on the ground."

"I stumbled over the stone and fell too," I said. "That's when I found the coin."

"Then our lack of coordination was to blame for my losing the coin and your finding it," Dad said with a grin.

"But for me, of all people, to find your cave— that's kind of creepy."

Dad nodded thoughtfully. "It is. Sometimes things just happen that we can't explain. That's what people probably call fate."

Meanwhile, it had gotten dark. When we went

into the kitchen, Steffi and Mom had supper almost ready. Fortunately, Mom didn't ask any questions. We were all very quiet—Steffi was obviously still mad. She didn't look at me at all, and she went to her room right after supper. I stayed at the table a while longer.

Right after Steffi left, Dad went into the living room to watch television. Suddenly Mom was standing beside me.

"Well," she whispered. "Did he tell you?"

"What?"

"The story of the doll and the teddy bear?"

"You know about that?"

"Sure."

"Does he know that you know?"

"I don't think so. Grandma told me shortly before we got married."

"Grandma knew about the doll and the bear?"

"Of course. She's his mother."

"And what do you think of it all—kind of dopey, huh?"

"Dopey?" she laughed. "No, not at all. Quite the contrary."

"Funny," I said, just before Mom left the kitchen. "Dad said that Grandma didn't know about it."

"Oh well, mothers and wives often know more than their sons and husbands think."

I'll certainly have to watch out for signs of that myself.

Now I'm sitting here in my room and thinking about things. Everything has already changed again. This morning at breakfast Steffi still wasn't talking to me. I tried not to look at her. In school, though, every once in a while, I had the feeling that she was observing me surreptitiously. Once she took a breath, as though she were going to say something, but then she didn't. Then, during recess she just talked that much more with Collin and Norbert. I couldn't understand what she was saying. I would have loved to know because they kept looking my way. Only once James walked really close by me during recess and grinned and grunted softly.

I wasn't hungry after school. I went right to my room. After a while I heard Collin. So nothing has changed, I thought. It was as though the last few days had never been. Even Mrs. Hansen had already called again.

But then there was a soft knock on the door.

"Yes! Come in!" I called.

Collin and Steffi stuck their heads into the room.

"Can we come in for a minute?" my sister asked.

"Sure. What do you want?"

"I was still pretty mad this morning that you scammed us. But then we were talking. . . ." Steffi cleared her throat and waited. Collin went on.

"So, all right. Steffi said that you were really right—that the business with the treasure map really wasn't a bad idea. And we did have a lot of fun, too. And when I think about how you two came running up with Fat Bertha . . ." He dissolved into laughter.

I always say it: I have a terrific sister.

"But the rest of it was my idea," Collin continued.

"What idea?"

"That we go on together. You see, I think Collin and Co. is a really cool detective agency, and we wanted to ask you if you'll still be in it with us. Norbert would be glad too, he said."

I really thought I'd misheard. Everything was a blur. Then somehow I managed to get out: "I'll consider it."

Steffi and Collin left again right after that. There really wasn't anything at all to consider, but I wanted to let them dangle a bit.

Soon I'll go across to Steffi's room and tell them I'll join Collin and Co. I don't have any idea what cases we're supposed to solve, but I'm sure something will turn up.